Sideline Ho

By

C. J. Domino

Sideline Ho

By

C. J. Domino

Slightly Ghetto Books
A Subsidiary of Shero Productions
Baton Rouge, Louisiana

Slightly Ghetto Books, P.O. Box 84066, Baton Rouge, LA 70809

Sideline Ho

Parental Warning: This book contains explicit language and descriptive sexual acts, which are inappropriate for individuals under the age of 18.

Edited by Novel Ideas:
sbdst05@hotmail.com

For information on booking the author for book signings and other events:

sheroproductions@yahoo.com

ISBN: 978-0-6151419-0-9

Printed in the United States of America

This book is dedicated to the memory of my mother,
Sarah Rodney Domino.
For believing in me when no one else would,
you will always be my shero.

"Character is what you are in the dark."
D. L. Moody

PRELUDE

What in the hell am I doing? What have I done?

As I lay in his arms, I cursed myself for allowing this to happen again. Instead of coming to my senses and kicking his ass out in the cold, I nestled closer. We were so close that I felt his eye lashes fluttering as he ended his post-sex slumber.

His hand glided across my tattooed hip as his fraternity-branded arm drew me in closer. I felt him growing next to me. His excitement matched my arousal as I spread my legs apart, encouraging his exploration.

He moved on top of me with ease, shifting his weight, careful not to crush my petite frame. We never said a word – didn't have to. As he entered me, my legs intertwined with his, pulling him in deeper and deeper. Our movements became harmonious, synchronized lovemaking.

Soaked in sweat, my pace quickened. I was about to reach my climax. He looked into my eyes, felt the raw emotions that were running between my thighs, and always the studious lover, he rose to the challenge. His thrusts adjusted to the steps of my pelvic dance. I moaned while clutching his ass, my nails desperately trying to draw blood.

I wanted to leave my mark, let her know that someone else had been creeping outside of her door.

My common sense went out the window. I forgot about the other people and the emotional baggage that we shared as my body shivered in blissful delight. Waves of orgasmic ecstasy washed over me again and again.

We collapsed into sheets that reminded me that purity had a color, even if I was living in sin. I blocked out the truth that screamed for me to get the hell up and run as far away as I could. Instead, my tongue found solace in the warmth of what was hidden behind his full, luscious lips.

Amazed that my body was still eager, I grinned as he began to plant soft kisses on my stomach. Just as his head began to disappear below my waistline, Marcus Houston's voice sang out from his cell phone – a subtle reminder that *she* was really his favorite girl.

Two Months Later

It was hard for me to concentrate on what was coming out of my best friend's mouth because images of that damn pink plus sign kept flashing in my head like a neon marker.

"Damn, Nikole, I just told you that Brian gave me crabs, and you don't have shit to say?"

Just as I was about to make a clueless response, I watched in amazement as Bebe retrieved a pack of Newports and a lighter out of her Coach purse. With her lips pulled in tightly, she tapped the bottom of the pack before pulling a cancer stick out of the slim white box. Creases had formed in the center of her forehead as she flicked her Bic a few times. She turned towards the window to watch a few of the restaurant's patrons in the parking lot.

Bebe hadn't lit up a cigarette in years, and to top it off, she knew better than to do that shit around me. She knew that my allergies and smoke didn't agree. Annoyed, I tried to detour the cloud that was drifting my way in another direction. *You would think she would take the hint, but no...*

She's sitting over there whining about Brian, and as usual, I'm here acting like the dutiful friend. The least she could do is show me some damn consideration.

What was so interesting anyway? I thought to myself, as I angled my body to glance out of the window as well, only to see a handsome couple exiting a midnight blue Escalade. Out of habit, I zoomed in on the man, who was the color of dark chocolate with a medium build. I assumed he was a former football player that had gone soft from not working out after his college career ended. My eyes traveled the full length of his body as I continued to take in all of him. His clothing made me suspicious. Flexing a diamond crucifix, starched-down jeans and a white t-shirt that was not tucked inside of his pants, even if it was a Hilfiger, it all screamed drug dealer. I'm sorry, but men just don't dress like that during the middle of the week, at lunch time, unless they are unemployed or engaged in some illegal activities. However, from the looks of his car, I would say that the brother had some potential. If I wasn't in my present state, my hand graced my still flat stomach, I may have approached him. The chick on his arm wasn't even close to being in my league. Dressed in last season's trends, she resembled a little girl instead of a grown woman, such as myself.

I continued to stare in his direction as he removed his fitted white baseball cap and ran his hand across his freshly cut fade. His dark brown eyes searched the parking lot and then the windows of the restaurant. It was as if he could feel me staring at him. Our eyes met, and I shivered as a chill ran down my spine. *Damn.* He smiled briefly before replacing his cap and taking the arm of his attractive, albeit fashion misguided, date as they walked towards the entrance of the establishment.

A cloud of smoke drew my attention back to the present and my depressed friend. I watched as Bebe, with her eyes closed, pulled a drag from the cigarette and exhaled. For a second, she reminded me of a junkie taking a hit. She was getting too much pleasure from that damn nicotine. She turned her attention back to me, but was greeted with a disapproving look. I could feel that my eyes were dry and my green contacts were beginning to stick to my pupils. I blinked a few times to try and generate some moisture and to refocus on Bebe and her never-ending saga.

"Now, what were you saying about Brian giving you something?"

"Brian is having an affair," She stumped out the freshly lit Newport, "and evidently this heffa is nasty."

I cut my almond shaped eyes at her. *Now I know she didn't just go there.* Hell, he ain't no saint, and this isn't the first STD that she's gotten from him, so why all of a sudden does a sista have to be nasty?! What about him?

"What makes you think that?" I asked in my feigned innocent voice.

Bebe quickly lit another cigarette and began to puff away while staring at me. I guess she was waiting for me to come up with one of my famous diagnoses about their situation, but hey, what do you say to your best friend when you're the reason that she's miserable this time around?

Whatever. I picked up my menu and began to look for something interesting to eat as I continued to fester about her little comment. *Nasty… yeah, I got your nasty.*

I avoided making eye contact with her. Inside, I was burning up. I wanted to tell her about herself. How, if she were on her job, then she wouldn't be having all of these problems with her man. Funny how some people can talk the talk, but they can't back it up when it comes time to walk the walk. Wonder what her Fun Party customers would think, if they knew the queen of sex was having her own issues in the bedroom? Then the seriousness of her revelation finally hit me. Did she just say what I think she did? I slowly closed the menu and looked up.

"He gave you crabs?!"

"As usual, you are too busy thinking about yourself to hear anything that anyone else has to say," Bebe rolled her eyes. "I was about to order another Blue Cosmopolitan. You want one?"

"Slow down, Bebe, and tell me if I heard you correctly."

"What? You're kidding, right?" Bebe raised her left eyebrow slightly. "I just told you that my husband of thirteen years is fucking somebody else, and you're telling me that I should slow down on the drinking?" Typical Bebe, always taking shit the wrong way. I didn't say a damn thing about her downing a Cosmo. *Hell, she probably needs two or three right about now.* Her scolding look switched to a polite smile as a waiter, who resembled Ice Cube, sat a fresh cosmopolitan on the table.

"Good afternoon. Will you be dining with us today?" All eyes were on me, as usual.

"If Bebe is paying," I smiled in her direction, but she just rolled her eyes at me, probably calling me a freeloader in her head.

"Yeah, sure, why the hell not," Bebe mumbled, as she grabbed her newly arrived drink with one hand and dismissed the waiter off with the other one.

"Well, my name is Kyle if you need anything." I detected a hint of attitude in his voice as he cut his eyes at Bebe, who was too wrapped up in her own world to even notice.

"Excuse me, Kyle, can you tell me what Kushi Yaki is?" I took the opportunity to ask.

"Sure, that's Japanese for grilled skewers," He flashed a dazzling set of pearly white teeth in my direction.

"Sounds like a position to me." Bebe deadpanned.

"You have to excuse her," I shot my friend a threatening glance. "She's having a bad day."

"No problem," He nodded towards me, completely ignoring Bebe's comment. "Ladies, if you need anything else just let me know."

Ice Cube smiled again before walking away with the slightest hint of a switch in his hips.

"He just set off my gay-dar." Bebe smirked.

"Mine was starting to warm up, too." I smiled back at her. "So, back to your situation."

"Know what we need in our lives?" She leaned across the table and whispered as if we were conspirators, her way of getting off of the subject. "Some good dick, that's what!

And from the way that man over there is staring at you, my guess is that he would love to give you some."

"Excuse me?" I rolled my neck. "You really need to stop while you're ahead."

"Stop, for what? Girl, God didn't give me all of this to just sit around, let it shrivel up and fall off waiting for Brian to bring his ass home at night," she used her hands to outline her... *Wait... hold up a second*, I thought, *was it just my imagination, or was Bebe looking a little pudgy today?*

"I need to start using what my mama gave me, and you need to stop acting like somebody's grandma and do the same," her frown returned.

"First of all, God didn't give you that body. Your plastic surgeon, Dr. Peters, with the help of your husband's credit cards did. Secondly, didn't you just say that within the last two weeks you've had an STD? So, I take it that you've gotten some dick recently. Hell, I would be running away from dick instead of trying to have it run up in me! And who said I wasn't getting any?" I rolled my eyes at Bebe. "You know Terrance keeps me tuned up on the regular, and when he's not available, then that dildo you gave me last Christmas does a body good," A deep seductive laugh escaped from my lips. I discretely tilted my head a little to the side and followed the direction of her eyes, knowing damn well that it was Mr. Sexual Chocolate from the parking lot. He was sitting across the room and the sparkle coming from his ear was almost blinding. *Man, this guy is iced the hell out.* He nodded and smiled at me again. *Damn, I was busted.*

Turning my attention back to Bebe, I said, "He's okay." I turned up my nose and went back to deciding on the most expensive dish with which to indulge myself.

"And what in the hell is that suppose to mean, Nikole?"

"Did you see what he was driving? He's probably a drug dealer, which is definitely not my type," I waved my hand in a 'whatever' gesture and continued to browse through the menu, knowing good and well that if he asked for my digits I would happily place them in his hands.

"When did you get some morals and became concerned with how a man makes his money?" She played with the mother of pearl necklace that Brian had given her last year for their wedding anniversary.

"Whatever," I glanced at the stranger again. "He could stand to work out a little…" I pretended to sum him up. "But overall I guess he looks alright."

"Alright? You need to have your damn eyes checked."

"Okay, so the brother might have it going on if he stepped up his wardrobe and lost the small love handles."

"Hell, I know that. If he was butt ugly, I wouldn't have bothered pointing him out to you." She smiled in his direction then had the nerve to wave. *What was up with all of the flirting? This heffa was going over board with this affair shit. I mean really, come on. She married a guy whose line name was Freak-a-zoid! Hell, what did she expect?* But I must admit, he does live up to his reputation. I smiled to myself as I remembered our last nasty encounter together. I took a sip of water to clear my throat and cool me off before commenting again. "Anyway, that man over there is with another woman."

"And when did that ever stop you?" Bebe leaned back in her chair and folded her arms across her massive breasts that were trying to burst through her pink Ralph Lauren shirt. She was probably wearing a pair of navy blue pants made by the same designer. *Speaking of stepping up someone's wardrobe…*

"Can we change the subject?" I sighed.

I swear, even though we have been best friends since the eleventh grade, Bebe can really get on my nerves, especially when she starts complaining about her less than perfect marriage. Before she started her own business, her whining mainly consisted of '*what gift should I get Brian's partner in the law firm*' and '*why hasn't the Junior League invited me to become a member?*' If you were a stranger looking in from the outside, you could never tell that her entire world was just a big façade. But after hearing the same broken ass record for thirteen years, I began to see why Brian was tipping out on her. The woman was obsessed with living the lifestyle of the rich and famous instead of taking care of home; especially her man.

A wanna-be bourgie, Bebe was the chick from the wrong side of the tracks that got a lucky break. She got the fairytale life that all girls dream of. I, on the other hand, the one who grew up with a silver spoon in her mouth, became a statistic.

She graduated from college with honors and married her high school sweetheart, whom, might I add, comes from a heavily endowed family. They live unhappily ever after in a beautiful estate on Dalrymple Drive that overlooked one of the magnificent lakes that surround the campus of Louisiana State University.

I'm a single black female. I'm still trying to get through my undergrad studies, and I come with a lot of excessive baggage, including a two-year-old son from a relationship with my on-again, off-again married beau. Besides our friendship, the other thing that Bebe and I have in common is that both of our men are certified hoes.

Looking up, I noticed for the first time that Bebe is looking a hot mess today. Her usually neat French roll is being replaced with a wild mess of curls that are hiding her makeup-less face. From the looks of things, she hasn't seen a pressing comb, or a hairstylist, in a hot minute. Her eyes are red and puffy, probably from crying about Brian all night. *And let's not mention her nails that are sporting chipped polish, and ohmygoodness... does she need a refill too?*

"Does Brian's cheating have anything to do with your new look?"

"Oh, yeah. That's right. You're the only one that's supposed to walk around looking cute all day in over-priced clothing and a weave that hangs down to your ass."

"Hold up sista," I put my hand in front of her face to stop the nonsense that was flying out of her mouth. "Did I do your ass something?"

I rolled my eyes and returned my hand to the table, right on top of the butter knife. I continued my rant, "Hell, don't get it twisted. Just because we've been friends since forever, don't think for one second that I won't get up from this table and jack you up, Bebe. I came here because you said you needed to talk, but I'll be damned if I'm going to sit here and let you insult me just because you're having problems in La La Land. Now, let's try this again. What's up with you and your man?"

Just as she was about to get to the point, Kyle returned to take our orders. In a hurry to have him gone, I picked the first item that I saw on the menu and rushed his ass off. I needed to know what was really going on between my lover and his wife, since it was becoming quite obvious that he had been lying to me.

"He got that trifling bitch pregnant." *Aw shit...* I thought to myself. She had cursed, which only meant one thing: she must be mad as hell this time around.

"Back up...what are you talking about Bebe?" I asked nervously, as I tried to calm my ass down a few notches. I slowly retrieved my hand from the silverware.

She took a deep breath, and then exhaled, "He's been having an affair for the last two months. My shit started to itch after we had sex about two weeks ago. I went to Dr. Williams, who confirmed that I had crabs, and now this... this... bitch is pregnant." *Now, I know good and well that my pussy is clean, and there are no unknown critters crawling around on me! Yeah...crabs go with cheap motels and crack head hoes. That low down bastard. Crabs! Oh, hell no! And wait a minute...he told me that he and Bebe had stopped having sex over a year ago*, I raged inside my head.

"How do you know all of this?" I put on my game face, just in case she had figured out what was going on between her husband and me.

"Are you deaf? I just told you! Fuck, never mind." Bebe frantically lit another cigarette, not realizing that she had never put the other one out, and took a drag as if her life depended on it. "I had him followed, hired a private investigator," she exhaled.

She wiped a tear from her eye, "Can you believe that he messed over me with some slender little thing with long, wavy hair that's streaked blond?" Bebe laughed.

"And...? What's so damn funny?" I self-consciously touched my hair.

"When the private investigator showed me the photos, I said to myself that his new ho looked a lot like you," she turned her head and stared me dead in my eyes.

"You're tripping." I nervously began to swing my chocolate-suede, Via Spiga booted leg under the table. I thanked God for small blessings, as Kyle returned to the table with our food.

"Anything else, ladies?"

"Not right now, thanks." I threw a fake smile in his direction before diving into my garlic shrimp and steamed rice. I didn't realize just how hungry I was.

"Yeah, I know," Thankfully, she perked up a little and gave me a genuine smile. "You're right... I am tripping. Anyway, I put his ass in the guest room until I can figure out my next move."

"Which is?"

"A divorce... I guess. Look, let's talk about something else. What took you so long to get here?"

Before I could answer her, my cell phone began to vibrate. With a mouth full of food, I answered against my better judgment.

"Hello?"

"Is there a problem?" the female voice on the other end asked.

"Excuse me?"

"I asked you a simple question. Is there a problem?"

"Who is this?" I asked after haphazardly swallowing the contents of my lunch.

"Who do you think it is?" *I'll be damned.* It just wasn't my lucky day.

"How did you get my number?"

"Don't worry about all of that. All you need to know is that I got it and you'd best believe that if you keep messing around with my husband, I'm going to use it and a whole lot more."

Click.

"Who was that?"

"Guess."

"Humph. Mercedes. What is it with you and Terrance? I mean, really. Why are you still messing around with him, especially after he dumped you for the Barbie Doll?" she inquired, as if I had asked for her opinion.

I jabbed a shrimp with my chopstick and plopped it into my mouth to keep me from saying something that I might regret.

"You know, you really should leave him alone before you, or somebody else, gets hurt. Hell, you need to be glad that Mercedes hasn't opened up a can of whip ass on you..." She took a sip of her diluted drink, avoiding my eyes. "I can't say that I would blame her," she continued, mumbling under her breath, before setting her glass down on the table.

"Mercedes isn't that crazy." I rolled my eyes at Bebe. She was really pushing my buttons today.

"Tell that lie to someone else. Remember, I was there when she ran up on you at that Hornets' game and tried to kick your ass, simply because you were there wearing a jersey with his number on it."

"Must you remind me?" I plastered on another fake ass smile, and then plopped some steamed broccoli into my mouth and chewed like crazy.

"Look, my life is just as fucked up as yours..." Bebe took another drag from her cigarette.

I coughed. Wasn't sure if it was from the smoke, the vegetable that had just went down the wrong pipe, or Bebe admitting that her life was far from perfect.

"So, what else is going on besides the obvious?" She sounded distracted, and as I peered up from the menu, I caught her rearranging her now lukewarm entrée' around on her plate. She hadn't taken a bite. At that moment, I regretted what I had done. It didn't matter that her husband was trifling. He was still her husband, and I was supposed to be her best friend.

"Do you still love him, Bebe?" I played with my chopsticks, nervously anticipating her answer. *Please let her say no, then maybe I won't feel so bad.*

"I'm not sure. I mean, what do you do when you've given a man your heart and soul, catered to his every need and fantasy, and he still goes out there and messes around with another woman? Look at you and Terrance. I still don't know how you do it, girlfriend. After he went out and married Mercedes, I thought you would have been through with him. I guess love makes you do some crazy things."

"Like staying with their ass after they've given you crabs?"

"Yeah, well, we have a lot of history together, both good and bad," she sighed. "I guess I need to figure out if the good out weighs the bad."

Bebe looked off for a minute, as if she was contemplating what she had just said. "So, you never did say what's going on with you?"

"Nothing much, just broke as hell." I answered, before shoving more food into my mouth.

"What in the hell happened this time?"

"Funding. I got an e-mail from my department chair informing me that the university had lost their accreditation and that they were no longer eligible for Pell Grants from the federal government. That also ended my student worker position in the research lab." I decided to keep the possibility of being pregnant to myself, at least for right now.

"What kind of mess is that? You don't tell people that kind of news in an e-mail. And when did you ever work on campus?"

"Now, see, you're worried about the wrong thing."

"If people would worry about doing their jobs correctly and stop trying to get over, then maybe the university wouldn't be in this predicament." She pointed that broken acrylic-enhanced finger in my direction.

This affair must have really gotten to her, because Bebe normally wouldn't be caught dead with her hands looking this torn up. Me? Hell, I keep my neighborhood nail shop in business. But what I still can't understand is why the sudden changes? It's not like Brian hasn't cheated on her before.

"And how did you come to that conclusion anyway?"

Rolling her eyes, Bebe explained, "It's called connections. You're not the only one who knows people. Hell, just watch the news; somebody is getting arrested up there at least once a month for some fraudulent activity. So, what are you going to do now?" She actually seemed concerned, and that was killing me.

"I don't know."

Bebe's pursed lips let me know that she didn't like my answer. She scolded, "Well, maybe if you would have graduated from college when you were supposed to, your dad wouldn't have cut off your funds, and you wouldn't be in this predicament."

"That's easy for you to say."

"Girl, please. I wasn't the one who grew up living like the Cosby's, remember? So don't give me that bullshit. You need to get up off of your ass, and do something, Nikole. Stop waiting on a certain Negro to leave his wife, and get on with your damn life. Besides…that shit never happens in real life." Bebe looked me in my eyes pointedly.

See, ooohhhh, let me calm down again. "Uh, hello! For your information, I'm not waiting around for Terrance, and I am trying to do something with my life!" I sneered at her. "What else do you want me to do?" *Hell, I wish she would stop acting like life is so easy, and get a grip her own damn self.*

"Are you sure none of Mercedes' people work in financial aid? I could see that maniac paying somebody to delete your information from the system."

"I wouldn't put it past her."

"Hell, if you were messing around with *my* husband and I had those kinds of connections, *I* would get your ass where it hurts, too," She paused and took a drag from her cigarette.

Bebe breathed deeply and seemed to regroup. "Or it could have been some sista who was just jealous of you. You know how we are… get mad because another woman looks like she is doing better than you are."

"Whatever, Bebe."

"Come on. What student walks around the campus of an HBCU wearing Vera Wang and stilettos and drives a BMW, even if it is fifteen years old? And even if you didn't walk around there looking like you had it going on, people would hate on you simple because of your people. Being the daughter of a retired judge isn't easy you know. Someone is always scrutinizing you, waiting for you to mess up."

"And how would you know about that? Look, what happened in the past is just that, the past." I replied.

"I bet…"

I had to admit that she did have a point. I couldn't help it if I liked the finer things in life. Shoes and clothes were my addiction, and for right now, men were my suppliers. When I changed my major for the fourth time and messed up my chances of graduating last spring, my daddy took away my credit cards. Well, just the ones that were in his name, and he cut off my living allowance.

"Last time I checked, that wasn't a reason to cut someone's financial aid."

"Well, if they think you are a spoiled brat that's got a trust fund stashed somewhere, then you don't have anything to lose."

"I am hardly a trust fund baby," I said, defensively.

"Yeah, yeah, yeah," she smiled. "If you would stop pissing off your old man, maybe he would give you your damn trust fund now and not make you wait until after he dies," she joked. "But you could call Brian. He may be a jerk, but he's also a damn good lawyer, sleazy, but good." Bebe took another drag. "He'd take his own momma to court, so you know he wouldn't have a problem with his alma mater."

"It's not about the money," I folded my arms across my chest.

"Girl, puh-lease," She exhaled a cloud of smoke. "It is always about the money. Oh...sorry," She fanned her hand, trying to clear the air. "Hey," She snapped her fingers, "why don't you come and work for me?"

Now it was my turn to look at her like she was crazy.

"...At least until you can figure out your next move."

"You have got to be joking."

"No, I'm serious," she smiled.

With a degree in chemistry, Bebe was the proud owner of Erotic Fantasies, a company that specialized in sex toys for the kinky adult in you, the only thing that brought her joy these days. I swore every time she talked about a new product she looked like she was having an orgasm. Makes you wonder why she, of all people, would be having marital problems.

"Look, all you would have to do is help Royce to organize the Fun Parties. It's simple."

"Nothing is simple with you, Bebe."

"The job is yours if you want it."

"How much are you trying to pay a sista?"

"How does a twenty-percent commission sound to you?"

"How much do you average?" Hell, she needed to give me some hard figures to work with.

"Around two grand." Bebe answered.

Now I wasn't a mathematician, but I knew that four parties a month equaled eight grand. If you let Bebe tell it, she was working at least two parties a weekend, and during the wedding season, she sometimes worked three. I was broke, so at this point, any amount sounded good to me. Fun Parties are a thriving business in these parts of the good U.S. of A. Unlike other parts of the country, here in Louisiana we can't have an adult novelty store on every corner, except in the French Quarters of New Orleans, and most of their kinky businesses were shut down after Hurricane Katrina roared through in 2005.

"Umm, I still don't know. Let me sleep on it."

"Honey... I know you're not going to sit around and wait on 'what ifs'?"

"Girl, whatever."

"Okay, okay. So, will you come and work for me, or do you want to put yourself in another situation where you're gonna get shafted in the rear end without any Butt Ease?" She waved her index finger at me, laughing.

"Bebe!" I was still trying to close my mouth from the shock of her comment. I mean, come on, I know she sells the stuff, but to hear that come out of her mouth! Not Miss Goody-Two-Shoes. Once I had recovered, I had to give it to her again, she was right. The university had messed over me in a major way, and I had just sat there and took it.

"Well, I hate to say I told you so, but I did hint that this was going to happen."

"Must you remind me?"

"So, I ask you again girlfriend. What are you going to do?"

Sucking in my breath, I answered, "No more butt fucks."

"Now you're talking!" She held up her hand for a high five, and I willingly obliged. "So, can you start tomorrow? My company's big annual Fun Party is coming up, and I normally bring in a few temps to help out Royce. I don't think he would mind one more set of hands, especially if they were yours."

"You want me and Royce to work under the same roof? You must be nuts."

"Come on! You, Royce and I are the Three Musketeers. He'd loved to work with you, and so would I," She smiled a devilish grin.

"Sure, why not. But don't say I didn't warn you if things get a little crazy."

"Baby, crazy is my middle name."

As we exited the restaurant, I found myself taking one last glimpse at the 'okay' gentleman, hoping that maybe he would flash me that gorgeous smile. To my surprise, he was engrossed in a conversation with his date; his hand was gently placed on top of hers as they shared what appeared to be an intimate moment. I shrugged my shoulders as I removed my Donna Karen sunglasses from my Gucci handbag and covered my eyes. I was satisfied with the brief encounter, and simply knowing that if I had really wanted him, I could have had him.

Chapter 1

Once I had left Bebe, I made my way over to my OBGYN's office to confirm what I already knew. After circling around in the parking garage for what seemed like forever, I finally found a parking space that wasn't too far from the medical plaza's entrance, for a normal person. Out of breath, and with my swollen feet starting to throb from the mini hike I had to endure, I barely made it to the fourth floor office.

Dr. Williams must have ripped her waiting area straight from a page out of Home and Garden Magazine, because the place was exquisite. The room was tastefully done in Queen Ann furniture; you felt like royalty every time you stepped through her office doors. As soon as I entered the door, the smell of mango hit my nose. I felt my stomach do a somersault. I groaned. This was the part that I hated about being pregnant, the sickness. I still don't understand why they call it morning sickness, because I swear I've never been sick in the damn morning. I pulled out a bottle of Evian water to wash away the queasiness. Hopefully, my stomach would settle down. *You would think that in an office in which pregnant women frequented, the Doc would choose less fragrant candles.*

"Hi, my name is Nikole Freeman, and I have an appointment with Dr. Williams."

The new receptionist greeted me with a funky attitude and a ton of forms. She looked familiar, but I didn't feel like trying to remember where I knew her from. I was hoping that the feeling was mutual; I wasn't ready for the entire world to know about my current situation.

"Do you need something else?" She checked me as she flipped open her cell phone.

"All of this information is already on file." I replied, as I peered at her from the top of my shades. My outstretched manicured hand was more than ready to hand it all back to her.

"Look…" She rolled her eyes to emphasize her point. "You can take that up with Dr. Williams. Now have a seat, and she'll be with you in a minute." She pointed to a vacant chair in the waiting area.

I wanted to tell that ghetto-fabulous hoochie that if she didn't like her job, she could always quit and let a sista like me take her damn place. Instead, I gathered up the forms and tried to be cordial with her trifling ass.

"Thanks," I stated with an expressionless face, but to my dismay she smacked her lips and began to chat into her cell.

"Girl…what was I saying? Oh… That was some stuck up bitch trying to be all that… Know damn well ain't no sun shining up in here with those space alien looking glasses on… What? Yeah, Girl…I hear ya."

A huge part of me wanted to turn around and cuss her out, but instead, I tried to be the bigger person by just ignoring her nasty little comment. I looked around and noticed rounded bellies of various sizes scattered all around the room. It seemed that today was set aside for all of the pregnant women in town. I watched as some stroked their stomachs, while others glowed, talking with their significant others about family things. It was too much. Feeling slight embarrassment, laced with a hint of jealousy, I sat in a corner, as far away from them all as I could get, and began to fill out the mound of paperwork that was resting in my lap.

Was I going to spend this entire pregnancy feeling this way? This was so messed up. This wasn't supposed to happen. We were just messing around, having fun, enjoying each other's company. I wasn't trying to get pregnant. Touching my stomach, I wondered about his family history? Was he related to any crazy people? And what about sickle cell anemia? *Shit...* Staring at the many blanks, my eyes began to water. *Too many damn questions that I just didn't have the answers to.*

As I sat there aimlessly trying to fill in the blanks, my mind began to wonder as I thought about the handsome stranger that I had encountered earlier today. I imagined him to be caring, thoughtful and considerate. I bet the mother of his unborn child would never have to go through something like this alone. I rubbed my stomach again as I tried to answer the remaining questions on the form.

My name was called, and I was told to take a pee in a cup. I was led to a cold examination room that smelled of alcohol. One wall displayed various pictures of a woman's uterus, while the other one was decorated with the pictures of children that Dr. Williams had delivered during the course of her medical career. The nurse reviewed my chart then gave me some instructions before she exited the room. After removing my clothing and putting on the peek-a-boo gown, I hopped up on the dreadful exam table, you know, the one with the 'feet hoisters', as I like to refer to them, and waited for the doctor.

"Nikole, what a pleasant surprise."

"That depends on who you talk to," was my flat response as I leaned back on the cold, crunchy paper.

In stark contrast to the cold sterile room, Dr. Williams was a vibrant, older black woman with a contagious smile. She had a way of making people feel at home, even though most of her conversations were held while she was perched down between your legs.

"So, we're back again, I see."

"Unfortunately, yes." I stared at the ceiling, hoping she would just hurry up and get this torture over with.

"And where is that handsome Terrance today?" she pried inquisitively, while examining my cervix.

"Who knows?"

"Did you see my niece, Moet, out front?"

"Oh… I thought she looked familiar. Wasn't she in nursing school or something like that?" I remembered Moet from my earlier years in college. We hung around the same people, but were never friends. I never liked her because she was ghetto, even back then, and her mouth never let you forget it. Moet was always talking shit, putting your business in the streets. *I sure in the hell hope that she doesn't remember me.*

"What?" Dr. Williams laughed. "With that nasty attitude, she's lucky to be working here. The only reason I'm giving her a chance is because she's my niece, but if she were anybody else, I would have fired her yesterday, and that was her first day here."

Not interested in talking about how somebody named after a drink got a lucky break, I asked, "So, how far along am I?"

"Well, according to the information you gave the nurse in regards to the date of your last period, you were right. It looks like you are around eight weeks."

"Can you check and make sure that I don't have any STD's?" Embarrassed that I even needed to ask her a question of that nature, I closed my eyes and prayed that her answer was no.

Dr. Williams' head came up for air, and I watched as she removed the rubber gloves that she was wearing and adjusted the wire frame glasses that graced her delicate face.

"Uh, Nikole, sweetheart… Everything looked normal," she paused, smiling nervously. "Well, I guess it's safe to say that you haven't been using condoms with Terrance, but if you are having some concerns about him having multiple partners, then it's up to you to protect yourself. No glove, then no love, especially since you're pregnant. You wouldn't want to put the baby at risk," She patted my knee. "Well, you know the routine," she said, perking up a little.

"I'll see you once a month, up until your last four weeks of the pregnancy."

"I'm not sure I'll be keeping this one," I blurted out, not sure where that statement had come from.

Startled, she stared at me. "Nikole, I know I'm just your OB-GYN, but is everything okay? Do you need to talk? "

"I'm just not sure this is a good thing."

"Honey, you're just nervous."

"No, it's not that."

"Have you and Terrance talked about this?"

"No," I shamefully admitted.

"Now, I know this isn't my place, but I've known you all of your life, and your mama and I go way back." She smiled, and I guessed she was remembering their years together as sorority sisters and college roommates at Xavier. "You and I have talked about a lot of things that have never left this office..." she paused, "Unlike other women, you have an abundance of support. You know that your parents would do anything to help you out. And your friends…well, you already know."

I smiled.

"Why don't we see if we can hear the heart beat?"

Dr. Williams squirted the cool, thick gel on my stomach before placing a flat-tip wand on top of it.

"This one is stubborn," She moved the wand around, but there was no sound.

"Is everything okay?"

Her smile became strained as she continued to listen for the heart beat of my unborn child.

"Dr. Williams… is there a problem?"

"I'm not sure. Look, it's perfectly normal. Sometimes we can't hear the heartbeat this early in the pregnancy, especially with a petite person like you but to be on the safe side, I'm going to have a few tests run. So, after we finish up, I want you to head to the lab, and then to the radiologist for an ultrasound. I'll write you a prescription for some prenatal vitamins," She patted my hand before turning to leave the room. I sat there for a moment trying to gather my thoughts. *Did I really want to have this baby, especially under the circumstances that it was conceived? And what if something was wrong?* Would I be prepared to deal with a child who may come into this world with a disability? Or did I want to call it quits, and run to the nearest abortion clinic?

As I struggled to get the paper gown undone, my cell phone began to vibrate inside of my purse.

"Hello?"

"Nikole?"

"Who else would be answering my telephone, Brian?"

"You've been real bitchy lately, what's wrong with you?"

"Nothing, why? What's up?"

"I was calling to see what you've got planned for tonight. Thought maybe we could go out for some drinks later on?"

"That would give us a chance to talk."

"Talk about what, Nikole?"

"I think Bebe knows."

Chapter 2

*N*eedless to say, Brian never showed up for those drinks and that 'talk'. It's been a few days since that conversation. I've left numerous messages on his cell phone, but he hasn't returned any of my calls. I've tried reaching him at his office, too. Clarrisa, his secretary, always claims that he's either with a client, or in court, before she slams the phone down in my ear. She's probably fucking him too.

To make matters worse, working for Bebe has turned out to be more difficult than I thought it would be. Feeling like a slave, I noticed that she worked the hell out of me my first few days on the job. Who would have known there was so much involved when trying to organize a Fun Party or selling sex gadgets? I keep reminding myself that this is just a temporary situation, but I can't help feeling like this position is so beneath me. Stationed in a small, stuffy, grey cubicle with furniture that's older than me, today my job consisted of filling the online orders and dropping them off at the post office.

All of the clerks smiled knowingly when I walked up with the heart-imprinted packages. I was out done. These people actually knew who Bebe was. It was as if they worshipped her. I was totally amazed, but the icing on the cake was the clerk who was waiting for me as I emerged from the post office with her order written on a slip of paper.

"Tell Bebe it's for Cheryl; she'll know who I am." I thought I was going to gag, but I just put on my happy face and shoved her little note in my Kate Spade bag.

I'm so immersed in the Wonderful World of Kinky that I probably will be having nightmares about plastic dicks and bondage kits tonight.

Exhausted, I couldn't wait to get home to the serenity of my African inspired apartment and my four-hundred-count Egyptian cotton sheets. My mom had volunteered to pick up my son, Omar, from his daycare, so I could have some time to myself tonight. First, I had to tackle my homework assignment, becoming familiar with a box filled with company products.

As I turned the corner approaching my apartment complex, I noticed the personalized license plate that read 'Nupe 1' on Terrance's '78 Cutlass. Annoyingly, it was occupying my assigned parking space.

All I want to hear is that he has my child support from the last three months. Financially, Terrance was usually very supportive of my son and me, but for the last few months he had been acting like a scrooge. One day I was on top of the world, partying in Aspen or lying on the beach in Hawaii, with money to burn. Then all of a sudden he cut me off cold turkey. Something about us needing to chill out for a while, because his wife had started to keep tabs on his spending and him not wanting her to get suspicious. I reminded him that if he would have married me, instead of her, he wouldn't be having this problem, and as usual, he just ignored me. But today I am pissed! Not only has he gotten skimpy with the child support, but he also hasn't made any attempt to pay my rent for the last two months, either. What I needed to do was cut his ass off. *Stop him from getting a taste of my sweetness whenever he pleased.*

So, why do I stay with him? Terrance was my man throughout high school and in college, and even though he married someone else, I still have a weakness for him. Unfortunately, he knows it. That son of a bitch, and I am not using that term loosely either, uses it against me every chance that he gets. That's how I ended up in this predicament, but today was going to be different. He was going to give me some answers and some money, or I was reporting him to the district attorney's office for non-payment.

Screeching to a halt, I tried to regain my composure, but my adrenalin was pumping. Before I had a chance to open the car door, my nosey neighbor, Mrs. Domaine, was knocking on the car window.

Dressed in a faded pink house duster, with pink foam rollers flopping all over her head, the woman is the definition of a 'hot mess'. A widower of two years her only companions were her dogs and soap operas. She only left her apartment when it came to her pets, or to report to the apartment manager the numerous arguments that Terrance and I have had over the years.

"What does she want now?" I say loud enough so that maybe she would get the hint.

"Hope I didn't startle you, honey."

"Not at all, what can I do for you today?" I cracked the window and immediately regretted it as the smell of 'old people' hit my nose, and my stomach began to quiver.

"Well, you don't have to make it sound like that."

"Sound like what?" Like, every time you come over here it's because you are pissed off with something that's taken place at my apartment. *No, never. Not Mrs. Domaine.*

"Anyway, I just wanted to let you know that Princess is pregnant."

"Congratulations," I replied. *Hopefully, a few puppies will keep your nosey ass out of my business.* But the frown on her face let me know that there was more to this visit. "I take it that you are not happy about your bundles of joy."

"Well, I think Prince is the father, and we need to discuss Princess' future medical bills, and what have you." She lifted one eyebrow at me.

Now I know this woman has just lost her everlasting mind, banging on my window, claiming that my prestigious pedigree has gotten her mutt knocked up! I took the liberty of climbing out of my car, so that I could look her right in the eyes as I shattered her bubble for once and for all.

"Now, how did you come to the conclusion that Prince was the culprit?" I folded my arms across my breasts and waited in delight to hear her theory.

"Well, they do go to the same groomer, and remember that day in the park when we caught him humping on Princess?" She twisted her mouth into an ugly frown.

"Umm…well, sorry sweets, but Prince had his nuts cut off a few years ago, so he is not the guilty party. Don't you have a male dog as well?"

"Well, yes, but he and Princess don't get along. I doubt if it was him."

"Why don't you check with your vet, and see about getting a paternity test done." *Jesus, I'm just as crazy as this woman, out here talking about some canine drama. This is insane.*

"I guess."

"Well good, I'm glad we got that settled. Now if you will excuse me," I stated, before turning to open the back door to the rental car and trying to retrieve the heavy box that was stashed on the seat.

"I'll let you know what happens." Mrs. Domaine yelled as she stepped back into the safety of her own place.

"You do that," Terrance replied, before I had the chance.

Chapter 3

*T*here he was, Mr. Missing-In-Action himself, the gorgeous, caramel-dipped, former NBA superstar, Terrance Barone was approaching my car. My man of steel was all that and then some. Sporting a silver hoop earring in his left ear and dressed in a pair of loose-fitting basketball shorts and a wife beater, I could tell that he had just finished shooting a game of hoops with his boys. After all of these years together, he was the only man who could get my panties wet just by being in his presence. I hid my delight as he strolled my way. He flashed the same million-dollar smile that had landed him several lucrative endorsement gigs over the years and also allowed him to wiggle his way into my panties any time that he wanted. I couldn't help but smile, too.

He had the body of a god, and I appropriately worshipped every inch of him. My eyes swept over all six feet five inches of his athletic body that was cut to perfection. Smiling a mischievous smile, I had to admit that my baby was looking too good. Today, his black curly hair was slightly tapered in the back and on the sides, and his fair face was sporting a two-day-old shadow beard. His piercing brown eyes twinkled in the sunlight as he leaned into me, his aroused manhood ready to taste my goodies. I took a deep breath. Had to remind myself that I was supposed to be pissed off at him…

"What's up?"

"I'm trying to get this box out of the car," I snapped, tilting my head back to take in the spectacular view. *Snap out of it, Nikole. This fool has been playing you, and here you are drooling all over him - AGAIN. Get a grip...*

"Doesn't look like it to me." His eyes swept across the inside of the vehicle. "Looks like you were out here talking to your messy neighbor. What did you do this time?"

"She claims Prince got Princess pregnant."

"Dogs need love, too."

"You would know." I checked him.

"I'm going to let that one slide. You need some help?" he asked, before reaching for the box that was nestled on my back seat.

"Sure, why the hell not," I stepped back from the dirty rental car. *Yeah, that's the least you could do since you haven't been living up to your other responsibilities,* I thought to myself, as I took in the rear view of him bending over to retrieve the box. *My goodness.*

As we entered my apartment, I began to laugh. Not because of the weird look that had crept across Terrance's face after he peeked inside of the box, but because of my lazy English bulldog, who was looking very pitiful. It seemed as if his eyes were begging me not to act a fool, or was that his hungry look? I was so tired, I couldn't even see straight, and Terrance's dumb ass was still standing there with the box in his hands. I guess he was waiting for me to do something with it.

"Thanks for the help, Terrance," I took the box from him. "I'll do it myself," I declared, before placing the box on the kitchen counter with a hint of attitude in my voice.

"From the looks of things, you must be working for Bebe now," He reached inside of the box, making a face as he pulled out a red glow-in-the-dark vibrator. "And how is the self-proclaimed hedonist doing these days? Oh, my bad, bourgie and sex freak don't go together," he laughed, as if that shit was funny. Why was he so worried about what I was doing, or where I was working at these days, anyway? *I tell you...the nerve of some people.*

"Excuse me? Why are you all up in my business? And put that thing down. I'm not trying to buy one."

"Why not? It might add some excitement to those lonely nights when I'm not around," He puckered his lips and kissed the air.

"And while we're on the subject, why haven't you been around lately?"

"Anyway..." he rolled his eyes, "why are you driving a rental car?"

"You're changing the subject." I folded my arms across my chest and waited for an answer. *No, my brother...you are not getting off that easily today.*

"See, that's why I don't like to come over here, because you're always fussing about something. I ain't trying to argue with you, Nikole. Not today." He threw his hands up in the air, his way of calling a truce.

"All up in my business, and how did you know it was a rental?" I huffed. "Maybe I decided to buy myself something new." I rolled my neck and pretended to stare off into space.

"Woman, please! Correct me if I am wrong, but I don't think a Hyundai Accent is your type of car. Where's the BMW?" He opened my refrigerator door and pulled out a carton of orange juice, careful to check the expiration date before his inconsiderate ass guzzled down the last of its contents.

"Terrance, all I want to talk about is George, Benjamin, and who ever else has their face on money."

"Damn, can't you cut a brother some slack, Nikole?" He walked towards me, but I took two steps back. I had to stand my ground, and be strong. *Damn, why was he wearing Dolce & Gabbana cologne? He knows that's my favorite fragrance on him. Damn, Damn, Damn...* He inched towards me again.

"Why are you really here, Terrance?" I tried to sound tough, but was sounding weaker by the minute. Sometimes I think he has put a spell on me, because no matter how hard I try I just can't get him out of my system. Even when I try to date other guys, I find myself comparing them to him, and in the end, they always fall short and end up getting dumped.

"Can't a man come over and spend some time with his son?" He reached out to stroke my hair, but I moved out of his reach. *Be strong girlfriend...*

"Oh, don't tell me you got some other nigga around here playing daddy." He had major attitude in his voice now. "I wouldn't put it past you to do some shit like that." And let the games begin, I thought.

"What are you talking about? Look, do you have my child support? It's a no brainer, Terrance, just answer yes or no." *Same shit, different day...when will this madness end?* You would think that he would have figured out the routine by now. Whenever he calls, I am always ready, willing, and able to cater to his every need. *So, why all the B.S.? And why now?*

"I know you ain't trippin about no damn money, girl." The muscles in his face began to twitch. Fuck, I don't care if he's getting mad. Maybe I should have ruffled his feathers a long time ago.

"Well, if you would keep a job, we wouldn't have this problem every month. Oh, I forgot, you don't pay child support every month."

"I bet you miss those NBA child support checks. Look at you, turning red. Yeah," he gloated, "I bet you are really heart broken that they can't garnish my pay checks anymore. Pissed you off when I blew out my knee, and I had to quit playing."

"What? Oh yeah, that's right... they did pay you to be a bench warmer, didn't they? You know what? Never mind, Terrance." All he wants to do is argue, and I'm trying to look out for the well being of our son.

"Naw, you all bold and shit. Say what's on your mind." His voice went up a few octaves. *Damn, had I pissed him off that much?*

"Like you said, I was just trippin, baby." I tried to smooth things over. Terrance was moving closer to me, and I felt my pulse quicken.

As he rubbed his stubble cheek, I studied the sexy diamond brand that was peeking out from under his shirt. *Why does he have to be so damn sexy?* I thought to myself, as I let my guard down, and Terrance continued to tell me about his money problems.

"It's kinda tight right now, so why don't you cut a brotha some slack." *Just when I was about to let his ass out of the doghouse.*

"Cut you some slack!? What you need to do is stop trying to be a playa, and get a real job!" I snapped.

"Who are you hollering at, Nikole?" I felt his hand constrict around my neck, and as I gasped for air, I tried to recall why I was still involved with this fool.

"You must have your people mixed up." He shook me like a rag doll before finally letting go.
I massaged my neck with one hand, as the other one instinctively went to my stomach. "If you know like I do, you would get yourself together."

"Look baby, I'm..." He moved closer, but I retreated by taking two steps back. I wasn't sure of his next move, and I wasn't trying to take any chances. In a split second, I watched as my world began to fall apart. His eyes traveled from my stomach to my eyes. *Damnit...he knew.*

"Nikole, don't tell me that you're pregnant again!"

"Do you have any money, Terrance?" I didn't mean for that to come out sounding like I was begging, but who was I kidding?

"How could you do this? Are you sure that I'm the father?"

"What?" *Who said anything about him being the father?*

"I don't believe this shit!" he yelled at me.

It happened so fast that I didn't realize that I had been slapped until my neck snapped back, and my face began to sting. *What in the hell has gotten into him?*

"I thought you said you were on the pill," he fumed.

"Terrance, will you let me explain?" I started to say something, but I quickly decided that I didn't need to upset him any further. I rubbed my face, trying to figure out how I could smooth things over, but the look in his eyes told me that he didn't want to hear anything else that I had to say.

"Explain? Explain what, Nikole?"

I watched as he reached inside of his pocket, "Here are a few dollars to help take care of your problem, but I ain't promising you shit if you decide to keep this one."

He threw the small bills in my direction, but I only looked at the money that was lying haphazardly on the floor. Although I was broke as hell, my pride wouldn't let me pick it up.

"Don't worry about it. You're doing such a great job with Omar, I wouldn't want to put any additional burdens on you." I mumbled under my breath.

"Whatever."

Okay...what in the hell had just happened? He was treating me as if I was just a trick, or better yet, one of his gold-digging groupies. But I refused to go out like that.

"No, it's not whatever, Terrance. Not this time." I spoke in a low voice. My eyes left his handsome face and focused on the red robin that was chirping outside my kitchen window. "You need to give me the child support that you owe me, or else..." I turned and stared at him with tears gathering in the corners of my eyes.

"What you need to do is stop playing, Nikole. Because the way I see it, you played yourself."

"Have it your way, but it sure beats going to jail."

"Don't you threaten me, Nikole." His index finger jabbed at the space between us.

"It's not a threat this time. Believe that, playa." I pushed his chest slightly, before putting some distance between us as I hopped up on the counter. I knew I was pushing my luck, but what the hell? He had already choked the shit out of me and tried to slap all of my teeth out of my mouth. What else could he possible do? I was tired of him walking all over me and treating me like shit. "Try me if you want to, but I will call those people on you in a second, so don't even trip, homeboy."

Terrance looked at me as if I had lost my mind. He reached inside of his pocket again, and this time he peeled off five one hundred dollar bills. "Here," He handed me the money. "Now, you need to handle that, and I don't want to hear shit about no damn child support."

Don't ask me why I sat there and continued to let this man believe that I was carrying his child. Sometimes money, or the lack of, can make you do some crazy things.

"Terrance, this isn't going to cover an abortion."

"You're right. It'll cover half, and since half of this situation is your problem, you need to figure out how to get the rest."

"I don't believe this bullshit. I bet when Mercedes came running to you, talking about how she was pregnant, you didn't tell her some bullshit like that. I know for a fact that you didn't question the paternity of that child."

"I'd better not ever hear you say anything about that situation again. Do you understand me, Nikole?" He pointed a threatening finger in my face. "You leave my wife and kid out of this!"

What kid? After they were married Mercedes claimed that she had a miscarriage, but if you ask me... I don't think the heffa was pregnant to begin with. Like I said, Terrance isn't that bright. Yeah, I knew that Terrance had been creeping around on me with her in college, but I also mistakenly thought I knew my place in his life. All of that changed when Mercedes started talking that pregnancy shit. To tell the truth, I've never been okay with the fact that he had chosen another woman over me, not after all the shit that I had done for him in the past. What really burned my butt was the fact that he cheated on me with some ole chicken head, ghetto-fabulous sista that could pass for white until she opened her mouth. I couldn't go out like that. I refused to let go of what was rightfully mine in the first place. In my mind, he was still mine. *My man*, and it was that thought alone that made me grow some balls.

"If I were you, I would move that body part. And you need to put your ho in check, and tell her to stop calling me."

"Yeah…but that ho is still my wife, Nikole."

Chapter 4

"**D**amn, Nikole, you are too sexy," Terrance moaned, before taking one of my 'girlfriends' into his mouth. *How in the hell did we end up like this?* I thought to myself.

During the course of him reminding me about his scandalous wife and blaming me for not being responsible and using birth control, we began our usual routine of kissing and making up. As I continued to sit on my Mexican-tiled kitchen counter, I gloated as Terrance showered me with love. Foreplay was always our favorite part, and we had been going at it for the last thirty minutes. I can't even lie; it felt damn good.

"We need to try out some of those toys you brought home," he whispered in my ear.

"Yeah, right. That would be a great way to learn how some of that stuff worked," My thoughts were soon distracted by the heated kisses that were being placed on my neck. Within seconds, my underwear was soaked, and my legs were wrapped around his familiar waist, pulling him in closer. I had to remind him of the passion that we shared. I had to prove to myself that I still had what it took to keep him coming back.

"Damn, baby, you acting like you miss me."

"This…is…messed up," I managed to get out, in between our heated kisses and panting. If it took fucking him all night to make up for pissing him off earlier, then that's what I would do. My love had no limits when it came to Terrance. There was nothing that I wouldn't do.

Unwrapping my legs, he slid his hand inside of my pants and then pushed them down towards my ankles. My vagina pulsed with excitement at the thought of him being nearby. I inched my legs open, giving him a lot of room to do his thing. Taking full advantage, he moved my g-string to the side with his fingers and slowly inserted one of them, then two, before he pushed me to a long awaited climax. I sighed with relief from his touches. The man knew how to make a woman cum, and that was my only concern at the moment. Sadly, I always found solace in our lovemaking.

We slid down to the floor, clothes thrown everywhere. Before I knew it, I was on all fours with my ass up in the air. I should have been ashamed of myself. I should have cussed his ass out when he hit me like that, but I love him so much. *I don't want to lose him.*

"Damn, Nikole, when was the last time that you had some?"

My only response was a low and deep moan, not because of the pleasure that I was experiencing, but to drown out any doubts that I was having. I tried desperately to fool myself into believing that what we had was really love.

"Sure you haven't been with anybody else?" he teased, while inching himself out of me.

"Like you care," I reached behind me, grabbing his ass and forcing him deeper inside of me. I needed him to make up for the pain that he had caused me, and not just for tonight. I moaned louder when he reached the center of my desire. *Right there, right...*

From the grunts that were escaping his lips, it was easy to conclude that the man behind me was enjoying every minute of our little escapade, too. As our sex noises tried to break the sound barrier, I heard little feet running across the floor. I froze for a moment, forgetting that Omar was still with my parents. Breathing a sigh of relief, I realized that it was only

Prince making an emergency exit. *Great, my dog will never look at me the same.*

"Baby, you know I want to be with you..." he panted, with a sly grin plastered across his face.

"I know, I know." This was such a lie that I barely had the nerve to reply.

Flipping me over, he began to rub on my g-spot while his mouth devoured one of my breasts. My body was telling me that it was exhilarating, but my mind was still clouded with doubt.

"Whose is this?" he demanded.

I tried to respond, but my mind was on instant replay as an image of him with his hand trying to squeeze the life out of me reeled through my head.

"I want to hear you say it," he whispered in my ear with an old familiar edge in his voice.

"You know who this belongs to," I purred back.

"Damn, Nikole, you feel so good," he moaned, while fingering my nipples. His voice dropped down an octave, "Say my name, baby. Who's your daddy?" He grabbed a hand full of my womanhood, before lowering his head between my thighs.

At some point, I managed to kick the abusive images of him out of my head and gave up one hundred and ten percent of my loving. I started by obliging to his request, singing his name in at least three different octaves before reversing the seduction. I felt powerful watching his eyes roll back in his head while my mouth savored his delicious flavors. I was all the woman that he would ever need...

"Damn, girl, what has gotten into you?"

"In a minute, hopefully, it will be you again."

Chapter 5

Sometimes it takes some wild x-rated sex to make a man come to his senses, or so I thought. I was more than happy to take a midnight ride when Terrance suggested that we get out and talk about our situation. Hell, I had convinced myself that if he wanted to believe that this was his baby, then I planned to let him. If he let me go through with the pregnancy, which I knew that he would, because his wife can't seem to have kids, then I would be home free, once I put him on child support. I stifled a giggle.

Terrance's offer to take me on a ride was definitely a good sign. After showering, I changed into a cute strapless Vera Wang summer dress and a pair of expensive sandals that he had purchased during our last trip to New York for fashion week. I hopped into his classic, and we took off. As we cruised around town, I decided to check my cell phone messages just in case Brian had decided to return one of my many calls.

"Who are you talking to, Nikole?"

"Damn! Nobody, Terrance," I huffed and turned my head to stare out of the window. *Stupid...* I should have just waited until he dropped me back off at the house. Now he's going to start tripping and asking all kinds of damn questions. *Do not act an ass, Terrance. Not now, not after what we just shared...*

I was hoping that he wouldn't ruin my high from our bomb ass sexcapade with some bullshit, and to my surprise, he didn't say anything else for the next ten minutes. Then, without warning, he reached across the seat and grabbed my Dooney and Bourke handbag.

"Terrance, what are you doing?" My stomach started to feel queasy, and it wasn't from the baby.

He didn't answer me, and I watched as his stupid ass threw my purse out of the window.

"What in the hell has gotten into you? Do you know how much that damn bag cost me?"

"Cost you? I paid for it, remember*?" Okay, here we go with the power trip.* I swear, sometimes I just wanted to drop kick him in his nuts.

"What? Oh, you've got issues tonight. Let me out of here," I demanded, while punching in the number two, speed dialing by best friend, Royce. I put the cell phone to my ear. *Damnit, why wasn't he answering his cell phone?* "And where the fuck are we, anyway?" I mumbled.

"Give me the fucking phone, Nikole."

"Hell no. I'm not giving you my phone," I switched the cell phone to my right ear. *This nigga is really crazy. And what if he tries to beat me up and leave me for dead?*

My thoughts were all over the place as I felt myself begin to panic. My heart felt as if it was going to leap out of my chest at any moment while the car quickly picked up speed. I looked around me, and all I saw for miles on end were long stretches of abandoned highway and pure darkness. With the top down on the convertible, the mist of early morning dew slapped me in the face as Terrance raced through the blackness.

Out of nowhere, Terrance reached across the seat and backhanded me in my mouth before snatching the phone from my hand. I watched, in horror, as he banged it on the dashboard until it began to fall apart. *Fuck!* I was pissed the hell off. I gritted my teeth. I wanted to tell him off, give him a good piece of my mind, but fear and common sense held my tongue.

"What's his name, Nikole?" He threw the useless gadget at me. *Oh shit, oh shit...what was I going to do now?* I went from being mad to scared shitless.

"Why are you doing this, Terrance!?" I was trying my best not to cry. Sweat was running down my back, and my hands were shaking uncontrollably. *Jesus Christ,* I thought to myself, *I really screwed up this time.*

"You think I'm stupid?" he yelled into the wind. "You think I'm fucking stupid, don't you, Nikole? I'm on to you... I know you've been sneaking around with somebody else!"

"Terrance," I was trying to sound calm. "You know damn well that I haven't been with anybody else." My voice was shaky as I lied to him again. I sucked on my throbbing lip, trying to ease the pain that had begun to magnify and creep across my entire face. At this very moment, I wanted to hurt him. I wanted him to feel the pain that I was feeling, but three times worse.

Fucking bastard busted my damn lip! I raised my hand to my mouth and could already feel the swelling. I carefully tucked the corner of my lip inside of my mouth to protect it from any further harm. What was I going to do now? The impact of his hand to my face had caused a low buzzing in my ears that had just now started to die down.

"You really expect me to believe that you're pregnant for me?" His eyes became cold as icicles as he punched the accelerator.

"Terrance!" I screamed his name as I grabbed the door handle. The car was now zigzagging dangerously down the dark and narrow road.

"Oh, you want to get out?" He swerved again before pulling into a new home construction site. "Then get out."

"What?!" I was terrified. A huge part of me wanted to run like I had gasoline drawers on in the middle of hell, but another part of me was mortified at being left alone in the

middle of God-knows-where. *Oh, he ain't just plain crazy...
Oh no, this nigga is certified.*

"If you know what's good for you, you'll get out of my
fucking car now!"

Hesitantly, I tried to exit the car, but as I placed one foot
on the gravel pavement, Terrance accelerated. This sent me
flying into the tiny pebbles headfirst. Fighting off the gravel
that was flying everywhere, I cradled my stomach,
frantically trying to get my bearings and stand up as he sped
off in the darkness. Feeling cold and utterly alone, I
desperately searched for his headlights while I wiped the
dust and tears from my eyes.

"I know he didn't..." I placed an aching hand on my hip.
I was still searching for some sign of Terrance, but it soon
became obvious that he was long gone and probably never
coming back. I tried to take a few steps, and that's when I
realized that the heel on one of my beloved Versace sandals
had broken off. Beyond frustrated, I yanked the sandals off
of my feet as the mascara and tears began to stream down
my face.

I couldn't begin to tell you what had pissed me off the
most: being abandoned, having my belongings destroyed, or
the realization that I had let this fool hit me twice in the same
night and done nothing about it.

Chapter 6

*T*ired from having walked five miles the night before, I struggled to get myself together for another day of selling lust. No matter how hard I tried, my heart just wasn't into it. After a few days of working for Bebe, I had grown tired of looking at battery-operated dicks and the sad face that she now wore because of the drama I had helped to create in her life.

Staring at my desk that overflowed with vibrators, batteries, fuzzy handcuffs and edible panties, I became depressed. Forgetting about my earlier reaction to the smell in the doctor's office a couple of days ago, I tried to lift my spirits by lighting some Coco Mango incense - maybe that would clear my head and help me to focus more on my work instead of the problems that I was facing in my own life. Just as I blew out the match, my partner in crime waltzed into the tiny grey cubicle with enough cheer to go around for everyone.

"Damn, girl, it sure smells good in here."

"What's up, Royce?" I looked up and smiled as his adorable baby face came closer.

"Gas prices."

That wiggled a laugh out of me. With the collar to his fitted lavender polo slightly up, Royce handed me a cup of coffee. He plopped down and crossed his legs in a worn grey office chair that was located next to my desk. To know Royce is to simply love him. Six feet of pure sugar - the brother is just too much.

"Um, I see Miss Thang is trying to look cute today."

"This old thing?" I tugged at the faded Slightly Ghetto t-shirt that I was wearing.

"If you say so...where did you get that one from?" He uncrossed and then re-crossed his legs in anticipation.

"Something I sketched up and had printed." I did have other talents besides shopping and messing with narcissistic men.

"Get the hell out of here."

"Something to keep me occupied."

"I thought that was Terrance's job." He rolled his eyes. "You ever tried selling those bad boys?"

"Naw, it's just a hobby."

"Such a waste. I bet you could make a few extra bucks selling them."

"You think?" I was surprised by his comment.

"Hell, you could be your own spokes model the way you are rocking that shirt with those tight ass jeans and those slammin' heels. I couldn't have put together a better outfit myself," he smiled, happy at his revelation. "So, has Mr. Terrance called to apologize about leaving your ass last night?"

It was just like Royce to bring up yesterday's news and then rub it in your face.

"No, not yet."

"And he won't. I'm telling you, Nikole, that man is a few marbles short. You'd just better be glad that I was able to put Charles on pause to come and get you."

"Damn, Royce..." I rolled my eyes.

"Don't roll your eyes at me, Nikole. I wasn't the one who left you stuck out off of Burbank. Shit, with all of these serial killers running around, you're lucky nobody knocked you upside your head."

Royce just didn't understand. Hell, nobody understood my relationship with Terrance. Everyone thought I let him hit on me and do all of these cruel things, but that wasn't it. Sometimes, I think it's the danger of getting caught by his wife that excites me, and other times I think it's the lifestyle that he lives, ballin' out of control, buying me expensive gifts, and taking me to exotic places away from boring old Baton Rouge. If I had a dollar for all of the times I'd said I was going to leave him alone, I would be rich. Changing the subject, I pointed to a stack of DVD's that were sitting on my desk.

"Ignore me if you want to, but remember I'm not the one dating Ike Turner," he rolled his eyes. "Anyway, I see you got those videos that I left for you."

"Those are porn movies."

"No, not really. They are more like 'how to' videos."

"What does that have to do with working here?"

"People want to know how they can incorporate these," he held up one of the vibrators that were casually lying on my desk, "into their sex lives."

"Baby, if I can't work with the real thing, then what's the point? That's just nasty," I turned up my nose in disgust, acting as if I had never used one before.

"Get a grip," he put the vibrator back on my desk. "You would be surprised to know who buys stuff like this." He placed a French-manicured hand on his hip. Royce continued, "It also helps to read some stuff that will get you nice and hot before a party. The look of lust is a killer sales technique."

"What!" *Okay, boyfriend was taking this just a bit too far.* I wasn't doing all of that to sell these stupid gadgets that women stick up their cats. *Puh-lease.*

"Girlfriend, you can't work up in here and not know about the kinky stuff."

"Did you smoke any illegal substances this morning?" I asked incredulously.

"Not yet, waiting until its time for my fifteen minute break. You want to join me?" He winked.

"It's a tempting offer, but I'll pass. So, Bebe tells me that the party we're organizing is supposed to be a big money maker."

"Honey, I don't know about you, but I will be there with bells on and my hand stuck out for my fat commission check."

"You can leave the bells at home." I smirked.

"Screw you." He shot back.

"Okay... so, what's the deal, Royce?" The commissions check comment had perked me up a bit.

"Shit. Bebe never invited you to her company's annual party? Each year she has a different theme. Last year it was 'One Wild Ass Night'. The name should say it all. Honey, she had inflatable dicks hanging from the ceiling, strippers working the hell out of a pole, chicks modeling lingerie (or the lack thereof), free food and drinks, and toys for days. People came from as far as Mississippi to hang with your girl. Shit, last year she made over five thousand dollars, and that was just from one night. And check this out," He leaned over as if we were conspirators, "this year she is planning to double that figure."

"Sounds like fun," I didn't mean to yawn, because I was actually interested in this part of the job. It was another thing that I hated about being pregnant. You were always tired.

"Could you at least act like you're excited?" He rolled his neck.

"Sorry," I yawned again. "But how can you stand to be around all of this stuff?" I swept my hand across my desk, settling on a vibrator that resembled King Tut.

"Chile, what better place to be than here?" he exclaimed. "I am in heaven!"

"That's exactly what I was thinking," I rolled my eyes.

"Stop being a party pooper."

I rolled my eyes at Royce again while inhaling the rich aroma of my toxic brew and taking a sip. "So, what's up with you and Charles?"

"Ummph," he grunted. "Do you want the long version or the abbreviated one?" *Oh Lord, why did I even ask?*

"That bad, huh?"

"Worse. Do you know that he doesn't want to go to California and get hitched!? I was like, look, I have been with your sexy ass for over ten months, and goddammit, you owe me this. I want a wedding like every body else," he pouted.

Royce had to be joking. Ten months wasn't nearly long enough to be making a decision about a relationship that could affect his life forever, but who was I to talk as I sat there and continued to entertain his madness.

"And what was his response?"

"Honey, he doesn't see the point. He claims that the shit isn't legal, and no sensible person in the state of Louisiana will honor our marriage anyway. And it still won't change the fact that at any time, we could be locked up for loving each other because in this sad state, getting some rear end action is still against the law. So, he's like, '*what's the point?*'"

Now, that was just too much information, but I knew better than to comment. "So, how do you feel, Royce?"

"Are you charging me for this shit? Because if you are, I want a damn discount since you haven't received your degree in psychology yet."

"You are crazy," I snickered.

"Hell, I know that."

"As desperate as I am for money right now, I should charge your ass," I laughed. Laughter three times in one morning, damn, Royce was good. Too bad he was taken and gay.

"I need to be charging you just for making your grumpy behind smile."

Just then, my office phone rang. Since the temporary secretary hadn't made it in yet, guess who had that new responsibility too? "Hold up for a second, Royce."

"Thank you for calling Erotic Fantasies, how may I direct your call?" I answered.

"Ah, yes, this is Melanie, from Financial Express, trying to reach a Nikole Freeman."

How in the hell did the credit card people find out that I was working here already? I wondered to myself. "I'm sorry she isn't in. Would you like her voice mail? Okay, hold please while I connect you." I pushed a couple of buttons and got rid of that headache.

"Okay, now what was I saying, Royce? Oh yeah, seriously, is this the final straw with Charles? Are you ready to cut him loose?" I asked him.

"I don't know, baby girl. We've been through so much. How do I just throw all of that away because that fool doesn't see the significance in us having a ceremony that is legally respected by some damn body, even if it is just for a little while?"

"I guess you are right."

Buzz, Buzz, Buzz!

"Where is the damn temp?" Royce asked, annoyed, as he got up to see who was trying to get into the building. As I took another sip of my coffee, Royce's voice boomed through my telephone speaker.

"Nikole, there's a super fine delivery man up here with a package for you."

An apologetic wave must have washed over Terrance, because before my eyes stood the sexiest man dressed in a form fitting, brown uniform. He was holding a box from Cingular Wireless, and in it was a brand new razor phone.

"Where's Bebe today?" the delivery guy asked.

"Locked up in her office, but I'll make sure to tell her that you asked about her, Sam." Royce was eyeing the poor guy as if he were a Hershey's bar with nuts.

I smiled as I signed for my package, and Royce smiled as he held the door open for Sam and watched as he made his way back to his brown delivery truck.

"Lord, it's going to be a good day today, because you let me have my eye candy," he joked, as he raised his eyes towards heaven.

"You are a mess." I pointed at him and shook my head, still smiling.

"So, Ike…I mean, Terrance must have broken your phone, again."

"How did you ever guess?" I twirled my new device around in my hand, admiring the color and its sleekness.

"I keep telling you that you need to leave his ass alone."

"Not now, Royce. Damn, give a sista a break!" I'd had enough of being lectured.

"Okay, I'll remind your ass when I'm standing over your grave at Roselawn Cemetery."

We returned to my desk where Royce and I continued to go back and forth about my relationship with Terrance for a good five minutes before the buzzer at the front door started to go off again.

"I swear, Karizma needs to get her act together before I fire her ass," Royce complained about the temporary secretary as he walked towards the lobby.

Sipping on my coffee, I decided to look over some papers that Bebe had left on my desk the night before. Suddenly, there was a loud shout and then the sound of high heels tapping quickly against the ceramic tile that covered the hallway leading to our work area. It sounded like someone was running.

"Hold up! You can't just barge in here like that! Bitch, I know you heard me!" Royce was screaming at the top of his lungs.

"Where the fuck is Nikole?"

"Shit!" I spilled a few drops of coffee on my jeans. I knew that voice. It was Mercedes, and from the words that were coming out of her mouth, she was beyond angry as she headed in my direction. *The Lord would bless Royce and forget about me,* I thought to myself as I sat there trying to figure out how I was going to handle Terrance's jealous wife today.

"What in the hell is your problem, and what are you doing here?" We had been going round after round since the day she stole my man, so unlike other women who sleep around with married men, I wasn't the least bit scared of Mercedes. Besides, she was all noise.

"Solving my fucking problem."

"And what problem is that, Mercedes?" I feigned stupidity for a moment as I picked up my mug and took another sip.

"You! You're my problem, Nikole," she fumed as she tossed a porn magazine that had sticky notes peeking out from the pages on my desk.

Royce finally made it to my work area, and he hovered near the entrance, watching Mercedes from behind. "I called security, Nikole. Ralph should be here any minute."

"Don't worry, I'm not going to fuck you up this time. But don't make this shit a habit," She pointed to the suggestive magazine that was lying on my desk. "I don't want to know what my husband does to you and with you." She took a step towards my desk, "And if you know what's good for you, you'd leave him alone." Her diamond-laced fingers were pointed like a gun and aimed in my direction.

"You don't scare me, Mercedes."

"Bitch, you need to be more than just scared of me. You're ass should be terrified, because I'm tired of you, believe that," she said, before pulling the pretend trigger. The sound of heavy footsteps broke the tension that had filled the small area.

"I received a call about a possible disturbance?"

"Yes, Ralph, but it was a false alarm," Mercedes turned around and batted her eyelashes at the Rent-a-Cop. "Next time, though, it might be different."

Chapter 7

*A*fter Royce finished cussing me out about the Mercedes drama, I couldn't help but take a moment to flip through the magazine that she had left. There were notes marking off pages that showed women giving men hand jobs and sucking their dicks. Others were strategically placed on the pages where women were fingering themselves and ejaculated for the camera while others sucked on their index finger leaving you to wonder where it had been only seconds before. I stared at the lipstick imprinted notes in disbelief. '*How many licks does it take to make Terrance cum...One-Two-Three*' and '*Every time you kiss Terrance you're eating me out*'. Leaving a detailed magazine with specialized cliff notes was definitely not my style. This was the handy work of someone else, someone nasty as hell. Sure, I had wanted him to hurry up and get a divorce, but I would never stoop this low. Hell, I had waited this long.

I began to get angry. *Was Terrance seeing some other bitch on the down low?* I mean it's not like I imagined him to be the most faithful person on this earth, look what he was doing to Mercedes with me. But it had always been a triangle between Terrance, his wife, and me. I had fooled myself into believing that he would come to his senses at some point and leave that crazy woman for me, but if he was getting some action from some other sneaky ass whore on the side, then there was no denying that my dreams were all lies. *The question was who?*

As I continued to flip through the pages, carefully studying the handwritten notes, I began to get this nagging feeling in the pit of my stomach. *Nooo, she would never do anything like this,* I thought to myself as I continued to stare at the erotic pictures and messages. *No way,* I assured myself, trying to laugh the silly thought away.

The morning's drama only magnified when Bebe's office door finally swung open, and she made her grand appearance for the day. I ditched the dirty magazine in my bottom desk drawer for the moment, and awaited her arrival to my cubical area.

Bebe stood in the middle of the main work area looking out of place in a pair of low-rise jeans, a white fitted dress shirt (that was a little too tight if you asked me) and a pair of stiletto cowboy boots that she could barely walk in. *What had happened to the conservative look?*

"Good afternoon, people. Royce, did you do the follow-up e-mails and phone calls regarding the party? I also forwarded some new addresses to you that need to be sent Evites. Did you get them?"

"Damn, slow down... I haven't checked my e-mails, and Nikole and I were just going over the list of things that needed to be done by this afternoon," he lied easily. "I still need to place a few orders with the distributors, and then ship out some products to customers. Nikole is going to do the Evites, in addition to the reminder phone calls to our guests." He turned to look at me, his eyes saying that I had better act like I knew what he was talking about.

"Sounds good. Nikole, how is everything going?"

"It's going," I replied, still reeling in shock over her wardrobe malfunction.

"Well, '*going*' isn't good enough. Did you get a chance to take a look at some of the products last night?" *What!?* She had her people mixed up today, talking to me as if I were some little peon.

"Sure did," I lied, while taking another sip from my 'Hot Mama' mug and trying my best not to cuss her out. After last night, and then the shit with Mercedes this morning, I was not in the mood to have someone snapping at me about some damn pussy products.

"Good. Royce will give you a quiz some time today, so we can get an idea on which areas you may need to brush up."

"A quiz?" *What in the hell was she talking about? This was a stupid job, not school.*

"Don't take it personal, sweetheart. This is my business, and friend or no friend; I need to make sure that everyone here is on the same page when it comes to my products. Staying on top of my game is the reason I make the big bucks." She tapped a fresh acrylic nail against her new Gucci handbag before giving me a knowing smile and sashaying out of the work area.

"And Royce, don't forget to pick up my dry cleaning, and grab us something to eat from Delpits Chicken Shack. It's going to be a long night," my girlfriend barked over her shoulder before we heard the buzzer for the front door, letting us know that she had left the building. *I was shocked that the vegan goddess wanted fried chicken, but who was I to complain?* Free food was right up my alley, especially now that I was eating for two.

"Royce, is she serious?"

"About the chicken or the test?"

"The test, Royce."

"Oh, as a heart attack. But don't worry. It sounds worse than it really is."

"Wow, thanks!"

"No problem. That's what friends are for. So, now, why don't you be a friend, and fix me another cup of coffee, so I can finish cussing your ass out," he stated in his best diva voice, while handing me his empty mug.

Chapter 8

I had just finished up another long day at Erotic
Fantasies and was packing up my stuff to head out of the
door when Royce busted my bubble.

"And where do you think you're going? I still need to
give you this pop quiz before Bebe has a cow. We've put
this off all day."

"Shit, can't this wait until tomorrow, Royce?"

"Hell, no. I'm not trying to lose my piece of a job behind
a test and you, girlfriend."

"Okay… What's the first question?"

"Oh no, baby girl, it's a computerized test," he laughed.

"Get out of here." My mouth formed a surprised 'O'.

"Hopefully, I will be, once you take it."

"For goodness sakes, let's just get this over with." I had
the strangest feeling that this was not going to be a cakewalk,
but hopefully my work experience from the last two days
would be enough to pass Bebe's stupid test.

"Everything is set up. Just click this icon to get started.
You only get twenty minutes to complete it. After that the
program closes, and the questions that were not answered are
automatically marked wrong."

"And I left the world of academics for this?"

"You haven't figured it out yet? Bebe ain't playing when it comes to her business."

"Hell, I can see that now."

"Well, good. Now, I'll be in the warehouse if you need me." He patted me on my shoulder, and then left the room.

When the first questions appeared on the screen, I knew that I was in trouble. After twenty minutes of struggling through fifty questions, I was sweating, frustrated and fighting off a migraine headache. Royce materialized in the room at the same time that the program clicked off. I heard a printer working in the background.

"Well, sugah, from the looks of these results, somebody didn't do their homework last night." He waved the computer print out as he approached me. "Terrance must have had you tied up," he snickered.

"That bad, huh?"

"To say the least," Royce shoved the results in my direction.

"Do I really need to know all of that stuff just to sell some fuzzy handcuffs?"

"That, and then some," He wiggled the papers again, before I snatched them out of his hand. "Look, it's late. I am trying to go and get my groove on, before heading home and having to deal with stuffy Charles. I tell you what… How about we forget that this happened? You get your butt in here bright an early in the morning, and we'll do a retake."

"Okay," I sighed. I was now convinced that working for my friend was a horrible idea.

"And to help you out, here is a copy of the study guide."

"There's a study guide? You mean, she made me take home all of that stuff last night, and there is a book that I can look at?"

"Don't take it personal; she does this to everyone. Besides, don't you think you need to know how a Micro-Vibro Keychain really works before you try and sell it to someone?"

"Give me that." I yanked the study guide from his delicate hands.

"Don't get bitchy with me. Blame your other friend. I would have given you the thing to being with."

"Sure." Just as I was considering the best way to kill Royce, Bebe came waltzing out of her office, where she had again been locked up the entire workday.

"Are you guys ready to roll?"

Royce snapped his fingers. "Ready when you are."

"Ready for what?" I asked skeptically.

"Our weekly girls' night out. Didn't Royce tell you?"

"No," I cut my eyes at Royce, "as a matter of fact, Royce is forgetting a lot of stuff these days."

Ignoring me, Bebe asked, "You didn't have plans for tonight, did you?"

I waved the study guide in the air.

"Besides the obvious, Nikole."

"Terrance might stop by later."

"And I know you're not going to be at home waiting on him, now are you?" *Actually, no… I'm going to be at home waiting on your man to come by, so we can figure out this pregnancy thing, Miss Attitude!*

"Well I was…"

"Hell! Over my dead body!" Royce glared at me.

"Nikole, come on. We haven't hung out in a long time," Bebe patted me on my back.

Royce glared at me, daring me to say something else about Terrance.

"What type of party is it?"

"There you go with all of these questions. Are you sure you're not studying law instead of psychology?" *And what in the hell was that supposed to mean?*

"It's a birthday party for some D. J.," Royce jumped in again.

"So, why are you guys going?"

"It's called networking, Nikole, and for the record, I don't care why people are there or who the guest of honor is. I just want them to leave remembering me and my business." *And you can't figure out why your man is never at home…*

Chapter 9

Royce and I rode together with Bebe following close behind. Whoever this party was for had to be a big timer, because they had rented out an entire restaurant to celebrate their birthday. We arrived at The Bone Fish Grill a little after ten p.m. Bebe announced that she didn't want us hanging all over her, and Royce didn't want any potential suitors to get the impression that he was straight, so we all went our separate ways, agreeing to meet up later.

Entering the party scene, the strong fishy aroma took me by surprise. After a few seconds my stomach settled down, and my eyes adjusted to the dim lighting. I began to take it all in, the slammin' music and the beautiful people who could have been walking billboards for every fashion designer on the face of the earth. The restaurant was divided into two areas, the bar room and the dining area. Tonight it didn't seem to matter where you chose to mingle because people were everywhere. This was really classy. I liked the birthday guest of honor already, and I hadn't even met him yet.

Bobbing my head to the lyrics of an old Salt-n-Pepa song that was my jam back in the day, I grabbed a glass of champagne, reminding myself that one was the limit for tonight. As I tried to maneuver my way around and blend in with this crowd, my cell phone began to vibrate. I glanced at the screen, which read 'UNKNOWN'.

"I am not in the mood for dealing with vindictive wives, a jealous baby's daddy, or any bill collectors, not tonight" I mumbled, as I clicked it off.

Scanning the room, I noticed that Bebe was right, there were some heavy hitters in here. "Maybe this wasn't such a bad idea."

I spotted some of the local music industries VIP's. I might not keep up with the stars, but I did have some knowledge about the movers and shakers. Boy Wonder was the DJ for tonight. I guess he was trying for a Renaissance man look, standing behind the turntables looking a lot like Mos Def. We made eye contact and smiled.

Wonder and I use to hang out back in the day. He was a nerd who had a thing for three things: music, weed and me. We were cool up until the day he gave me a joint laced with LSD, which put an end to our friendship and my smoking. I hadn't seen him in a while, but Royce and I listened to him every day on FLEX 100. Wonder had skills, but I preferred his counterpart, DJ Blaze, whom Royce and I jammed to during the early part of our workday. Over the airwaves Blaze sounded luscious, but he was probably ass ugly in person.

He motioned for me to join him. As I moved across the room and made my way to the DJ booth I noticed that this thugged-out brother sporting a diamond grill was vying for my attention. I checked him from head to toe.

Oh no, my brother, you have definitely got your people mixed up if you think you can step to me. I turned up my nose, a visible sign of disgust towards his kind, and kept walking, pretending not to have noticed him at all. Unfortunately, my plan didn't seem to work, because just as I began to ascend upon the stairs towards Boy Wonder, my male groupie cut me off.

"Uh, excuse me," I put my hand on my hip. "You're in my way." *You no-class-having, wanna-be-hood star.*

"Say girl, why don't you let me holla at you for a minute?" He leaned over, trying to whisper in my ear. Now you know I had to check his ass.

"Sorry boo, but you need to find somebody in your league," I looked him up and down before walking around him. "Because I ain't the one."

"*Bitch*," he spoke under his breath, and with his best gangsta strut, he moved on to his next potential victim.

"What's up, baby girl," Boy Wonder placed his headset around his neck, "you still giving brothers a hard time?" *You wish*, I thought to myself.

"Why you playing?" I hit his arm playfully.

"Where you been hiding with your fine self?"

"Handling my business, homeboy. What about you?"

"Chillin'. Your boy Royce is around here somewhere, and I thought I saw ole stuck up Bebe." He looked out into the crowded restaurant, gesturing with his head towards the areas where he had last seen them.

"Hey, don't talk about my girl like that."

"You know I ain't lying." Boy Wonder laughed. He flipped a switch to start his second turntable with one hand and reached out and pulled me in for a hug with his other. It slid past my waistline and grazed the top of my ass. From the bulge that was developing in his pants, I think it was safe to say that Wonder was very happy to see me.

"You know better than to play with me like that." I gave a coy grin and pushed away from him.

"So you're still playing hard to get after all of these years, huh, Nikole?" A look of disappointment had replaced his cocky smile from earlier. *Yeah, you'd better recognize that I'm still the shit and can still be picky when it comes to men.*

"I don't know what you are talking about," I flirted.

"I'm talking about us. You wouldn't give me the time of day back in college because you were so into what's his name... Kenneth?"

"Terrance."

"Whatever. You still with that loser?"

Look who's talking? You're just a DJ, and he's a baller, baby. You've got it twisted, Wonder. Better leave that purple haze alone, 'cause it's fucking up your brain cells, for real.

He leaned in closer so I could get a whiff of his chronic halitosis. I hadn't noticed before, but his breath was reeking, probably from smoking too many blunts.

"Look, a brotha is on top of the world now. I've been doing some work with Royal Records, and I recently signed a contract with Trill Entertainment. Even did some tracks for Lil Boosie and the Ill Relatives, and I know you've heard me on the radio. Girl, you need to be rollin' with me!"

Struggling to comment while holding my breath, I said, "That's real cool, Wonder." *Whoa, what you need to do is invest some money in dental hygiene, my brother.*

"You still ain't feeling me, huh, Nikole?" he pouted, like a baby.

"Now, why are you trying to handle me like that?" I smiled, while puddles formed in the corners of my eyes. *Lord, let me get away from this boy before I say something that's really going to hurt his feelings up in here tonight.*

"Maybe we can go out sometimes. Catch up," he continued to beg. *Man, the one thing that I hate is niggas who beg for the pussy.*

"Oh look, there's Royce," I lied. "Well, it was nice seeing you, Wonder."

"It's Michael."

"Huh?"

"My name is Michael."

"Yeah, right. Okay, see you around, Michael," I mumbled, while sprinting from the stage area.

As I briskly walked away, I heard Michael dedicate the next cut to his 'homegirl', and Chingy's voice came booming through the speakers: *"Damn girl, how'd you get all of that in them jeans, them jeans, how'd you get all of that?"* I didn't know if I should have been insulted or flattered.

Out of breath, I continued to make my way around the room, now searching for Bebe, when my eyes connected with an attractive gentleman. Recognition settled in quickly. I smiled, and then abruptly turned away. It was the guy from the sushi restaurant, the one who wore the white tee in the middle of the day.

"Damn," Looking down, I became pissed realizing that I was walking around with a shirt on advertising that I was slightly ghetto.

As I attempted to move deeper into the crowd, there was a slight tap on my shoulder.

"Now, you're not trying to avoid me, are you?" The smooth voice summoned me to stop.

Spinning around to make sure that the voice was talking to me, I spilled some of my drink in the process. Up close and in person, the man had a lot more potential than I'd given him credit for the other day.

"Oh my..." *Great, I sounded like a retard.*

"Excuse me?" He looked at me as if I really were crazy.

"Look what I did to you!" I exclaimed, as I motioned towards his leather Polo jacket. He was looking real fly tonight in his leather and jeans ensemble, which consisted of another white tee, a pair of white Jordan's and an iced out Fossil watch. He had switched chains; this one consisted of a diamond microphone, which was nestled nicely in the center of his well sculpted chest.

Looking down, he noticed the mess that my drink had made on his outfit. "It's actually my fault. I didn't mean to startle you."

"I am so sorry," I mumbled while trying to wipe off his jacket with my bare hand. *Damn, now I looked like a retard too, and to top it off, I was probably blushing.*

"Do you always blush when you spill your drink on people?" He appeared amused.

"No," I mustered. *Yup, I looked like a real idiot.* "Let me get a napkin," I stammered.

"Don't worry about it. I won't melt, besides I'm enjoying the closeness." He touched my hand lightly before directing me to the nearest table where we both took a seat.

"So, what's your name?"

"Nikole, and yours?"

He sipped on his drink, ignoring my question, and then he asked his next question.

"So, Nikole, where's your date tonight?" He looked into my eyes, patiently awaiting my answer.

"Actually, I am here with a friend." I began to bob my head to the Prince cut that was filling the airwaves.

"A friend, *meaning...*?" He checked our surroundings; I guess he was making sure that my 'friend' didn't run up on us.

"What?" I laughed as I swayed my upper body and snapped my fingers. This time he appeared amused at my enjoyment in the music. "No, no... man, oh goodness... Royce and I are coworkers."

"I see you're a Prince fan, too." He flashed me that million-dollar smile. "So, where do you work?"

"At Erotic Fantasies."

"You don't look like a stripper." He gave me a weird look.

"Stripper...naw, it's a company that hosts Fun Parties or as Royce would say 'sells sensuality'." I nervously gulped some of my drink, trying to figure out why I was blabbing all of my business to this smiling stranger. "So, are you going to tell me your name?" I asked before finishing off my drink. *Damn, I was only supposed to have one.* I really wanted to kick myself in the ass for that. My baby was going to be born with fetal alcohol syndrome or worse, if I didn't slow my roll.

"Of course," He motioned for the roaming waiter. "My name is Jackson."

"So, where is your date from the restaurant?" I playfully glanced around the room.

"Oh, Susan? She's around here somewhere. She's supposed to be doing a live remote. And for the record, we weren't on a date."

"Damn, somebody important must be celebrating their birthday tonight." I flipped my hair over my shoulder and looked around trying to spot the guest of honor. I ignored his last remark about Susan, because I really didn't care. She wasn't a threat to me. Besides, after tonight, she would be nothing more than a faded memory to him, because women like her never measured up to someone like me when it came to fulfilling the needs of a man.

"I guess that depends on whom you ask," he responded to my statement with a smile.

After our drinks arrived, I opted for water with a lemon this time, we talked for a while about music, books and food. I divulged a little more about my current employment dilemma and myself but what shocked me was that he actually appeared interested. Most guys start to get this far away look in their eyes when the conversation stops centering on them and becomes about you.

"If I hear of any opportunities that I think you might be interested in, I'll definitely give you a call." *What!? This was too good to be true.* I found myself aroused by his compassion and consideration. Besides my daddy, no other man had ever done something for me without wanting something in return, which was usually sex. *This guy was a gift from God.*

"So, how are you going to call me when you don't have my number?" I shamelessly flirted.

"Trust me, I'll have it by the end of the night," he flirted back.

As we continued to get acquainted, I heard a familiar piercing, shrill scream. It was Royce, and before I knew it, he was standing in front of our table, ogling my companion, with his hand extended out for a shake.

"Nikole is so rude! Hi, gorgeous, I'm Royce Wilder." Jackson stood as he took the extended hand and offered an

embrace as well. I liked that. Most heterosexual men act
like they have a problem with Royce.

"It is a pleasure to meet you, Royce Wilder." He released
a genuine laugh.

"Did I interrupt something?" Royce asked, hand on his
hip, looking like the Diva all the ladies want to be when they
grow up. "Anyway, are you single?" Royce continued.

My eyes went straight to the ceiling. *God help me,* I
silently prayed.

"You could say that," Jackson replied as he stared at me
with that sexy smile still on his face.

"Well, I am sure Nikole has told you that she is free as a
bird, but if she ain't your type, honey," he winked, "then,
you can definitely call me."

I briefly reconsidered murdering Royce.

"Well, I am flattered, Royce. Not too many people would
look out for their girl like that," he stated, while looking
directly into my eyes.

"What is this, the Love Boat?" That would be Bebe, and
by the looks of things, she was well on her way to being
wasted. I tried to hide the smile that was creeping across my
face as she attempted to walk in those stiletto boots.

"Looks like a love connection to me," Royce chimed in,
snapping his fingers. I just stood there, not believing that
this was actually happening to me, of all people.

"Nikole, isn't that the guy from the restaurant?" she
slurred. Without giving me a chance to answer, she fired off
another question. "So, Nikole, are you going to introduce me
to his sexy ass or what?"

"Bebe, you already know who he is," I hissed.

"No, I don't," she snapped back at me, which made her
sway in her stilettos. *That's good for you. Next time I hope
you bust your ass.*

"Jackson." He reached out, and shook her hand.

"Girl, and he's a gentleman, too? You better put him on
lock down, before some body snatches him up." Her eye
contact became suggestive. *What in the hell was up with all
of that? She had a man, even if he was a ho.*

"Wait a minute. That voice," Bebe snapped her fingers. "I've heard it before."

"At the restaurant, Bebe." I gave her some attitude back. I hate it when people walk around acting like they know everything.

"Hell, he didn't say anything!" She shot back with a little more attitude than before.

"Maybe on the radio," Jackson interrupted us.

"Please, shut up before you two scare the boy off!" Royce teased.

"Seriously. I know that voice." *Okay, Bebe, we get the damn point.*

Royce stopped joking long enough to concentrate on his boss' latest revelation and the hint that Jackson had shared with us. I just stood there staring at the two of them in total astonishment. He was such an ass kisser.

"DJ Blaze, from FLEX 100, the disc jockey that plays all of the old school music," Bebe snapped her fingers again.

"And you know it," Jackson laughed.

This could not be happening to me. The voice that triggers me to have mini orgasms on the way to work, in the car, or while I'm jamming on the job, is not standing here trying to get with me. *Thank you, God.*

"Get the hell out of here!" Royce screamed. "Happy Birthday!"

"Thanks, man."

"You know, Nikole and I are your biggest fans. Tell him, Nikole!" Royce panted. "We listen to your show everyday."

Still smiling, Jackson turned towards me to confirm what Royce had just shared. I was too busy wondering if his facial muscles ever got tired from smiling so much.

"She forgot to tell me that, Royce."

"Damn, Royce, do you know how to be discrete?" Bebe interjected.

"Spell it."

Just as Royce and Bebe were about to get into a heated discussion, the room was filled with the sounds of the next song: *"We fly high, no lie, and you know it... Ballin'..."*

"Aw shit, that's my jam!" Royce exclaimed, popping his fingers and swaying to the beat. "Come on Bebe, let's dance."

As they shimmied towards the dance floor, Jackson reached for my hand. "So, are we hanging tonight?"

"And you know it."

Needless to say, the night was all that and then some. As Royce gathered up Bebe, who was now slurring all of her words, Jackson continued to be a gentleman by walking us to my car. I looked up at all of the beautiful stars that were shining down on us. It was a magnificent night to dream. *What if he really liked me for my personality in addition to my looks? What would it be like to be in a drama-free relationship with a nice, caring man? I wonder if he likes kids.*

"I had a wonderful time tonight, Nikole."

"So did I."

There was so much heat passing between us that someone could have cooked a meal right there on the spot.

"Can I see you again?" he asked.

"I don't know, can you?" I teased.

Jackson moved in closer.

"You tell me," he whispered in my ear, before leaning back and looking into my eyes. I tried to search his eyes for a clue as to his next move, but before I could anticipate anything, his fingers intertwined with mine, and he placed the most sensual kiss upon my lips. I swear, my body was tingling from head to toe, but the moment was brief as Royce and Bebe came staggering towards the car.

"This is not my car." Bebe struggled to free herself from Royce's hold.

"I know, sweetheart. You're riding with us."

"Looks like you're going to have your hands full." Jackson commented, while shaking his head at the sight of my intoxicated friend.

"Tell me about it."

"Look, you get her home, and we'll talk later." He took my face into his hands, and then sealed the promise when his tongue parted my lips and explored the inner makings of me.

"Call me," I whispered, as Jackson released me and turned to walk away.

Chapter 10

"*B*ebe, where is your house key?" Royce asked, as he fumbled through her purse. We had been sitting out in front of her house for the past fifteen minutes, looking for this fool's house key. Let me tell you, I was beyond frustrated.

"Damnit, Bebe, answer me." Royce glanced over at the passenger seat, and that is when he figured out why he was not being answered.

"I don't believe this, Nikole. She is passed out," he whined. *Would you please stop the whining, already?* I rubbed my temples. I felt a migraine coming on as I remembered that I had forgotten to give Jackson my phone number. My emotions quickly switched from frustrated to pissed off.

"Royce, yelling and getting upset is not going to get us anywhere, and besides, can't you see that it doesn't matter?" I glanced over a Bebe who was curled up on the front seat of my rental and slobbing everywhere.

Royce leaned into the back seat and let out a long breath that I didn't even realize he had been holding in. "Nikole, this is not how I had planned to spend my evening." It was written all over his face just how upset he was. In the meantime, Bebe stirred in her seat, and Royce continued to mess with her, trying to make her wake up.

"Bebe, get up." I pleaded. But she didn't move. *Why was this mess happening to me?* I was ready to go home and chill the hell out.

"Girl, if it wasn't for her heavy breathing and the smell of alcohol, I would bet hard earned money that she was dead over there," Royce tried to fan away the awful smell that was starting to fill up the car.

"This is not the time to joke, Royce!" I yelled in frustration. This was some high school shit. Grown women were not supposed to go out and get this wasted.

"Okay, so what should we be doing?" he responded, agitated.

"Why don't you try rolling down your window, instead of rolling your neck at me, and give me the damn purse? Maybe I can find her house key." Reluctantly, he handed me Bebe's purse. "It's not like her purse is huge. Maybe I just missed it." He hesitantly gave in to my request.

I stuck my hand inside of the Gucci bag that resembled the one that I was carrying when I met her for lunch the other day. *I don't get it...why is she mimicking me? The tight jeans, stilettos and now this?* Moving from left to right, I searched the compartments quickly. As I reached inside of the last section, I felt the miniature African head that was her key chain. Pissed, I pulled out her house key.

"Don't look at me like that. I just told you there was a possibility that I missed it," Royce whined.

"Spare me, Royce. Can you help me get her into the house?"

"Do I have a choice?"

I was just glad to be getting Bebe out of the rental car. The new car smell had been masked with the stench of alcohol and Angel perfume, a reminder of her "Desperate Housewife" days of trying to sell Avon. Royce and I struggled to get her out of the front passenger seat, but before we could move her, she made a gurgling sound, convulsed, and then vomited all over the door. *Oh my goodness...*

"Shit!" Royce screamed, as he jumped back, letting go of her arm.

I tried to get a better grip on Bebe, but it was useless as she slouched over the car door, looking like a rag doll.

"Move, Nikole..." Royce finally replied, as he picked Bebe up and waited for me to open up the door to her house. Royce proceeded up the walk way as I looked on in amazement. I never realized just how physically fit he was. I guess I just always assumed that because he had feminine ways, he also had our limitations, too.

"Thank you, Royce," I huffed, out of breath, as I unlocked the door.

"We should have just left her ass on the door step." Annoyance filled the air around us as Royce continued to gripe and complain.

"Royce, we can't do that. And anyway, where is Brian? I didn't see his car outside."

"She didn't tell you? Girl... Brian moved out almost two months ago."

"What!?"

As I thought about the new knowledge that Royce had given me, my own stomach began to feel queasy. *Had I caused that much confusion in their lives? And why did she lie to me about him sleeping in the guest room?*

I gave the door a little push as we stepped into the elegant foyer of Bebe's home. As my eyes took in the small area, I realized that Bebe had done some redecorating. The small space was done in a rich gold tone and filled with an antique armoire. The floor beneath us was a rich cherry wood. It all screamed "money". I instructed Royce to dispose of Bebe in her family room, another richly done area.

As I walked through the large estate that she and Brian had purchased only a few years ago, jealously filled my heart. If Terrance and I would have gotten married, this could have been me living in a place that resembled the homes on MTV Cribs. Bebe had made her husband spend a grip on this place. I can still remember how upset he was when she first suggested that they move from their modest home on three acres in the suburbs of Baker to this magnificent home that overlooked a natural lake on the other side of town.

After I covered her up with a pink and green throw, we quickly exited the house. I was still filled with envy as I returned to the rental car. The rental company probably had pictures of me hanging up in the post office by now.

As I opened the car door, the horrid smell of vomit reminded me of Bebe's greatest flaw, not knowing when to stop.

"How am I going to get rid of this funk?" I tried wiping away the residue with some handy wipes that I kept on hand for Omar, but the site of gushy liquid began to make me feeling a little queasy again.

Royce shot me an evil look. "I don't do throw up, so I hope you're not expecting me to help you." He folded his arms outwardly, showing his rebellion towards the subject. My stomach began to quiver, and suddenly, I turned and relieved it of its contents before acknowledging Royce.

"This car is jacked up, Royce," I wiped my mouth with a fresh wipe as I held on to the door for support.

"Are you okay?"

"Hell no, I'm not okay! Look at this shit! Hell, look at me!"

"It's a rental car, Nikole; does it really matter?"

I took a deep breath before responding. I was on the verge of cussing this Negro out. "Would you want to drive around smelling acid processed foods and mixed drinks?"

Reading the look that had registered on my face, he quickly conceded, "Hand me those wipes." He reached for the container and attempted to wipe up the mess.

"Look, just get this car detailed in the morning, and bring the bill to work. I'll make sure the company covers your expenses."

"And the quiz?" I raised my eyebrow in anticipation of his answer.

"Damn, you sure do drive a hard bargain, but seeing that you have been through so much, how about I just leave the answer key next to the computer when you do your re-take?" He gave me a feeble smile.

"Sounds fair," I stuck out my hand to seal the deal with a shake.

Looking at my hand, but refusing to touch it, "Ah, no need to shake on it... just take my word for it."

As we were leaving Bebe's home, Brian pulled into the driveway next to us. He waved as he exited his sparkling new Benz, but I pretended not to notice him. It was too late.

"Nikole, when did he buy that?" Royce cocked his eyebrow towards the new toy.

"Who cares," I mumbled, as I put the rental in reverse.

"Nikole put the window down." Brian tapped on the driver's side window, smiling as if he hadn't been avoiding me ever since I told him we needed to talk. I looked over at Royce, who shrugged his shoulders, before I commanded the window to come down with the press of a button.

"What's up, Brian?"

"Royce, man, what's going on?" Brian extended his hand through the car in an attempt to make contact with Royce.

"Hanging out with the girls," Royce's cordial laugh was suddenly annoying. "I thought you had moved out?"

Brian shifted around nervously as Royce let out what was supposed to be private information. *That's good for your ass,* I thought to myself.

"Yes, Brian, what are you doing on this side of town?" I raised an eyebrow of my own, daring him to give me an honest answer.

"Look, I'm going to swing by later. I just needed to grab a few things." He lowered his voice so that only I could hear him.

"We've got to go." I felt my foot getting heavy on the pedal as I peeled out of the driveway. *Now you want to talk. It's a little late for all of that, don't you think?*

What could have been a perfect night was slowly turning into a disaster. As I clicked my cell phone back on, the message light warned me that my screwed up night was about to get worse.

"Hi, this is Stephanie from Budget Rental, and we are calling about our Hyundai Accent. We have left several messages. It is imperative that you return this call, or our car by two-thirty p.m. tomorrow afternoon, or we will report the vehicle stolen. Thank you, and have a nice day."

Chapter 11

$\mathcal{B}$rian showed up at my apartment around three in the morning, looking like a lost puppy. Since I'm a sucker for dogs, I went against my better judgment, and let him in.

"What were you doing at Bebe's house tonight?" I demanded.

"I'm still paying the house note, so technically, it's mine." His reply was a little too cocky for my taste.

"Don't give me that lawyer mumbo jumbo." I folded my arms and turned away from him.

"Nikole... you know that I love you, right?" He reached out to touch my arm, but I moved out of his reach. I was tired of the lies and not just from him, but from Terrance, too. *Damn, I never meant for things to go this far.* Now I'm stuck in one hell of a situation, and all he can think to say is, 'You know that I love you?' I didn't want him touching me, at least, not now.

"Don't say things that you really don't mean, Brian."

"What...? Admit that I married the wrong woman? Follow my heart, and try to make things right between us after all of these years?" *And here we go with the bullshit...*

"Brian, that was over twenty years ago. We were in high school. I know you're not still trying to hold on to that. You need to let that shit go."

"Just like that? Just let my feelings for you go, baby?"

"Go home to your wife," I snapped.

"You're gaining weight," He reached out to touch me again, but this time I didn't pull away. I shivered as the air hit my skin while his hands slid under my oversized t-shirt, lifting it away from my body.

"Bebe said that you gave her crabs, Brian. Is that true?" I wanted him to tell me that she was lying. I wanted to believe that what he was saying was really true. He did love me, and this wasn't just another fling for him, or worse, a fuck. I wanted so desperately to believe all of that.

"Bebe is upset because I moved out. You know how she likes to play the victim and get all dramatic when things stop going her way," he whispered in my ear, as he proceeded to give me a booty massage. "It's been a long time, Nikole...." As he pressed into me, I felt his manhood growing hard.

Sighing, I moved my neck to the side as he began to nibble on my earlobe. I was dick-matized. Want to know just how crazy I was about his six inches? I knew that it had been exactly two months, five days, and eleven hours since we last hooked up.

Now here's the killer part, Brian and I had this on again, off again relationship that had been going on since high school. The really pathetic part about our affair wasn't that his wife was one of my best friends, but that he and Terrance were boys.

We're all friends: Brian, Bebe, Terrance, Royce and I. But Brian and I have always had this special bond. We clicked from the first day that we met. Bebe liked him so much, and I was with Terrance, so we just put our feelings aside. That is, until the night Brian caught Bebe in a compromising position with some loser named Craig McKay under the bleachers at a homecoming dance. Devastated, Brian landed on my doorstep. After some consoling in my parents family room, one thing led to another, and Brian walked away with my virginity. So, no matter how much I try to let go, he's just as hard to get out of my system as Terrance. Sickening and pathetic, I know.

No one knows what happened between us. It's our little secret, and every now and then, we get together to scratch those itches that we just can't seem to get rid of. But this go-round, one of us slipped up, and shit happened.

"Brian, I'm pregnant."

I felt his hands retreat from my backside.

"Did you hear me, Brian? I'm…"

"I heard you, Nikole." His voice was as cold as ice.

"So, what are we going to do?" I turned to face him.

"We can't do this, Nikole." His mouth began to move in slow motion.

Suddenly, I felt like Jada Pinkett Smith in the matrix. *What in the hell was he talking about? Didn't he just say that he loved me?*

"What do you mean, 'we can't do this?'"

"What about Bebe?" he asked.

I moved away from him, and angrily began to pace the floor. "You weren't thinking about her two seconds ago. So, what's the problem now?"

"For goodness sakes, Nikole… Bebe is supposed to be your best friend!"

"And she's supposed to be your wife, but that didn't stop you from creeping over to my crib every now and then to get you some, now did it?" I placed my hands on my hips as I rolled my neck at him. He wasn't getting out of this that easily.

"Okay, Nikole," He was now standing in front of me. "What if we had the baby? How are you going to explain this to Bebe? Hell, to your family?! What are you going to say when the baby comes out looking like me, Nikole, or better yet, it doesn't look like Terrance? Then what, Nikole?"

I dropped down to the bed. I pictured all of the scenarios he had mentioned. Why hadn't I thought it all through before? Defeated, I knew deep in my heart that he was right.

Brian sat next to me, and repeated softly, "We can't do this, Nikole."

"I know," I whispered, as the tears began to stream down my face. Reality had finally caught up with me.
Brian held me in his omega branded arms as I continued to cry. He tried to kiss away my heartache, but some how, lust crept in and got the best of us, as our passion began to explode. Like I said, two months is a long time.

Chapter 12

"You must not know 'bout me..." Beyonce startled me from my sleep, as I frantically reached for my cell phone. Lying next to me, Brian began to stir.

"Hello," I whispered.

"Hey, girl, it's Bebe." I thought I was going to shit on myself when I heard her voice on the other end of the line.

"Shit... I mean, hey girl, what's up?"

"Are you okay?" She sounded a little too concerned.

"Yeah, sure. Why?" I asked, nervously.

"Because you sound weird. Anyway, I was just calling to say thank you for having my back last night."

I let out a huge sigh. "No problem, that's what friends are for, right?" I swung my legs out from under the covers and sat on the edge of the bed. *What time was it anyway, and why was she really calling me?*

"Are you sure you're okay?" *Didn't I just answer that question?*

"Yeah, look, can I call you back in a few minutes?" I glanced over at her husband, who was sprawled across my bed. The only thing separating us was air and some expensive ass sheets.

"It's Jackson, right?"

"What?" What was she talking about now?

"Girl, this is Bebe you're talking to. I saw how Jackson was all up on you last night. Is he all up in you now?" She laughed into the phone. "Go ahead, have fun. We'll talk later." I heard the smile in her voice as she told me goodbye and ended our call.

Talk about feeling like crap. And just as my call was disconnected from Bebe, Beyonce got cranked up again. *Why was everybody calling me now?*

"Is this a bad time?"

I smiled, because this time it was Jackson. "No, not at all. How did you get my cell phone number?" Naked, I tiptoed into the bathroom for a little privacy and closed the door behind me. I plopped down on the cold toilet seat.

"Bebe gave it to me a few minutes ago when I called Erotic Fantasies."

"Bebe?" *So, she knew that he wasn't over here.* Yeah, I've got to keep an eye on her. I'm definitely not giving her enough credit.

"Yeah, from the way she looked last night, I was surprised when she answered the telephone at the office this early in the morning."

"Umm... good ole Bebe."

"Well, I was headed to a meeting at the radio station, and I just wanted to check on you, make sure you were okay, and let you know that I was thinking about you."

A warm tingly feeling began to consume my body. *Damn, he called just to say 'hi'.* By knowing him for just this short of a time span, he had already managed to make me feel special.

"Well... uh... thank you for calling." I couldn't believe that I was tongue tied. Or was I still in shock that Bebe wasn't as naive as I thought she was?

After I hung up with Jackson, I thought about the man who was warming my sheets and what was the best way to get him out of my apartment. I just didn't want to deal with the slew of questions and 'what if's' that were sure to come.

I lightly touched my stomach and then reached for the doorknob.

As I opened the door, my eyes frantically searched the empty bed and then traveled around my cramped bedroom. He was gone, and I couldn't help a part of me from feeling betrayed. I really thought he would have stuck around and tried to help me figure this shit out. But before I could finish my thoughts, the scent of his lingering cologne mixed with our body chemistries had me making a mad dash to the toilet.

After my porcelain dive, I brushed my teeth and tongue, then I began to search the medicine cabinet for something to relieve my brain of the horrible headache I had just inherited. I made a mental note to ask Dr. Williams if it was normal to be having all of these headaches. I was probably stressed the hell out.

While popping two Tylenols, I thought about what Brian and I had talked about and the phone call from Bebe. Even in the morning, he was still right. There wasn't a chance in hell that I could continue to go through with this pregnancy, and my instincts were telling me that Bebe was on to us.

Prince had managed to make his way into the master bathroom with me and was on my heels. As he sat on the floor, looking at me sideways, I began to feel some remorse for my actions. "Stop looking at me like that."

Prince just cocked his head to the other side, as if he was thinking, '*...and why the hell not?*'

"Come on; let's go find you something to eat," I rubbed between his ears. Hopefully, that would remind me of my better qualities, such as being a loyal owner to my pet. I threw on my t-shirt from last night and together we headed downstairs.

I couldn't complain too much. If it wasn't for Royce dragging me to the party last night, I wouldn't have run into Jackson again, and believe me, he was well worth the misery that I was feeling now. As I stumbled downstairs, I heard moaning coming from the downstairs bathroom. I stared at Prince.

"Brian?" I called out, but there was no response. "Well, go on, and check it out." I tried to nudge Prince with my foot, but instead he moved behind me.

"I knew I should have gotten that German Shepard," I looked behind me to scold him, but Prince looked at me as if to say *'fuck that!'*

"Prince, this is what you get fed to do, check things out," I could have sworn that my sweet little doggy rolled his eyes at me before bolting back up the stairs.

There was a bang, and then something fell. Startled, I frantically searched for a weapon. The nearest object was an African spear that was mounted above the door. Grabbing it, I waited for the person on the other side to make a move. The door swung open, but before I had a chance to stab the hell out of my intruder, out tumbled Royce. I know I must have looked disappointed, realizing that Brian had really bailed on me.

"Shit, what in the hell are you trying to do? Kill me?" He was shielding his face with his hands.

"Royce, if I was going to attack you with a spear, it damn sure wouldn't be in your face, and what in the hell are you doing here, anyway?"

"Remember, I rode home with you," Reluctantly, he let his hands fall by his side.

"Sorry, I forgot."

"You scared the hell out of me, Nikole," He whined and began panting to catch his breath. "I thought you left out a few minutes ago."

"You're hearing things, Royce," I replied, hoping he would stop whining and believe me.

"That man has got you fucked up in the head." He finally smiled.

"What man?" I returned the spear to its resting place, trying to hide my paranoia. If he had been here all night, there's no telling what he had heard.

"Jackson. And by the way, why are all of your light bulbs burned out? I was in here knocking shit over trying to find the mouthwash."

"Shit." I raced to the front door, only to see the man from the utility company driving away from my unit. I slammed the door and stormed back into my apartment.

"What?"

"I forgot to pay the bill."

"And I thought I was doing bad."

"Royce!" I glared at him.

"Does Terrance know that you have his son sitting in the dark around here?"

"If he would pay his child support on time, then maybe we wouldn't be having this little problem."

"Um, well, if I were you, I would have taken his ass back to court a long time ago. See, you let this go on for too long with Terrance." He wagged his finger at me.

"Royce, don't start, and besides, they just cut my electricity off. Omar is staying with my parents, so he will not be sitting around in the dark. Even if they did cut the lights off yesterday, we were too blasted to realize that they weren't on, remember?"

"I don't remember you being tipsy." He flicked the bathroom light switch off and on several times. "But it does look like you need some help to me, sweetie."

"I said I forgot to pay the bill." I snapped at him.

"Nikole Freeman, there are a couple of things that you don't forget to pay in life. One of them is Entergy," he pointed to the light switch. "I swear you and Bebe are just alike sometimes."

"Don't you compare me to her," I became defensive. Prince barked at him. Okay, my loyal dog had returned to my side now that the danger had dissipated. I smirked at him.

"And… what are you two going to do? Double team me and kick my ass? Girl, please! I am a diva. Divas don't get beat down. Believe that!" He snapped his fingers, before moving from the bathroom door threshold towards the entrance to the patio to open the mini-blinds. "Anyway, if you needed some help, why didn't you just ask?"

"Thanks, but no thanks. Besides, the apartment manager is having me evicted. I have until the thirtieth to move out."

"Newsflash, Nikole... It's the fifteenth, and the diva is already busting his ass trying to plan this party for Bebe." Being all dramatic, he clutched his chest.

Silence.

"I'm pregnant." I blurted out.

"Where is Ashton Kutcher with his fine self?" Royce looked around my living room area as if there was a hidden camera somewhere.

"Royce, what are you talking about?"

"Heifer, either I am on *Punk'd,* or still drunk, because I know you didn't just tell me that you're pregnant and about to be evicted!" He was all in my face yelling, like I was hard of hearing, or just had some bad understanding.

"I'm afraid this isn't a joke, Royce." I moved him out of my space.

"Lord have mercy, Nikole... What exactly are you going to do?" He began to fan himself as if he were having a hot flash.

"The hell if I know." I swear this damn man could win an Oscar with all of this performing that he was doing up in here.

Royce shook his head and took a seat on my sofa. He patted a space next to him. Obediently, I took a seat while we both sat in silence for a few moments.

"Did you tell Bebe about any of this?"

"For what?" I looked at him like he was crazy.

"Nikole," he glared, "because she is your best friend."

"A little." *Hell, we'd better hope that she doesn't find out about any of this, or she won't be my associate, let alone best friend.*

"What's a little?"

I tried to change the subject. "That Budget Rental Car has put out an APB for me."

"Lord have mercy...Jesus Christ!" *Now why'd he have to go and involve the Lord and Jesus?*

"Royce, you know that I can't tell her everything."
Prince barked in agreement as I shot both of them
threatening looks.

"Why not?"

"Please."

"Please, my ass, girlfriend! You are the one acting like
she has lost her everlasting mind. Look, sweets, you are flat
broke. The eviction situation is a dead giveaway, and then
you drop a bomb on me about being pregnant."

"Don't remind me." Did he have to do an instant replay?

"Well, she must know that something is wrong, because
other wise, she wouldn't have let you in on her hustle." *Or
she's just keeping her enemy close to home*, I thought to
myself before responding.

"Something I never imagined myself doing in the first
place." I rolled my eyes.

"I never understood your relationship with her, anyway."

"What are you talking about, Royce? Bebe is my girl." I
started to get nervous. *What in the hell was he talking about
now?*

"She was a nobody in high school, a nerd. You let her
into our circle. We made her a somebody, Miss Popular.
Now, she's on top of the world, and she treats you like dog
doo doo. You just follow behind her, and kiss her ass, I
mean… why?"

"Can we change the subject?"

"Whatever, Nikole…" He dismissed me with a simple
wave of his hand.

I pouted in self-defense.

"Trust me, darling, that face doesn't move me, and you
need to remember that Erotic Fantasy is just a means to an
end. It's called a job."

"I am not supposed to be selling sex."

"Actually, that's called prostitution. You're selling
sensuality. There's a difference." *Sex, sensuality… what's
the damn difference?* I thought to myself.

"You are really into this."

"I am into the money, not Bebe, and not trinkets in my bedroom."

"Yeah, yeah, yeah," I yawned. I hoped this tired phase would pass. I had just gotten up, and I was exhausted already.

"So, when is the baby due?"

Silence.

"Okay, let me try a different approach." Using his perky voice, Royce asked, "So, Nikole, who is the father?"

"You wouldn't believe me if I told you."

"Try me."

"Brian." I laid it on the line.

"I need a drink." He fell into the cushions of the sofa. There was more silence between us. "You guys never stopped messing around, did you?" He looked at me skeptically.

Okay, so I lied when I said no one else knew about us. No one else knew about Brian and me, except Royce. What? I had to tell somebody.

"You must like drama because if Bebe ever finds out… I don't want to be around, because it's gonna be on and poppin'." Royce took a deep breath before continuing. "Okay, so… When are you moving?"

"I haven't gotten that far yet."

"Well, it looks like you need all of the help that you can get."

"Tell me about it," I sighed before glancing out of my patio door just in time to see the same bird from the other day fly away. Maybe that bird was a sign. Maybe somebody was trying to tell me that I needed to get as far away from this mess as I possible could.

"So, what's up with you and Charles? I noticed that you weren't in a rush to get home last night." I ventured. This was the perfect opportunity to change the subject.

Royce rolled his eyes, "Same story, just a different day. Now, enough about me, back to your problems, honey. What exactly are you going to do?"

"Bebe gave me an advance, and Terrance decided to take care of his kid this month, in addition to giving me the money to have an abortion."

"He thinks you're carrying his baby?"

"I guess. He started going off on me, and I wasn't about to stop him, especially when he started throwing money around."

"No, you didn't want him to use you as a punching bag, so you kept your mouth shut."

"Whatever, Royce," I rolled my eyes at him again.

"Don't '*whatever*' me, Nikole. Terrance shouldn't be hitting on you, and you need to put a stop to it, like yesterday."

"That's easier said than done, Royce."

"I'll remember that when I'm writing your eulogy." Tired of hearing the same death lecture from Royce about Terrance and his temper, I sighed and continued. "Anyway… I have enough money to hold me over for a while. I just need to figure out if it will be enough for a deposit and the first month's rent on another place."

"Why don't you just pay what you owe here and stay?"

"I already thought of that. The landlord wants me out. Said he's tired of the noise complaints that he keeps getting from the other tenants."

"I don't follow you?"

"Complaints about Terrance and me arguing and fighting."

"Damn, Nikole." He took a deep breath, "So, are you going to have the baby?"

"I'm not sure." I placed my hand on my stomach. After last night, it looked like an abortion was my only option.

Royce looked at me as if I had lost my mind. He knew how I felt about those things, especially after having gone through one in the past, but his words were different. "Well, you can't figure in the abortion money if you don't know what you're going to do about your living arrangements. And what is this shit about Bebe giving you an advance? Please! Bebe has money to burn, and besides that, you guys are friends. She was supposed to help you out with no expectations in return, not garnish your paycheck to get her money back. See, that's what I mean about her treating you like shit."

"Yeah, well it's not like I'm the most loyal friend, Royce."

"I totally agree. That was some scandalous shit that you pulled."

Mixed with shame and frustration, I dropped my head into my hands. "I can't work for her anymore, Royce."

"Forget about working for her, what about your friendship? Nikole, you slept with her husband, and now you're pregnant for the guy," he paused. "Both of you had better hope she doesn't find out."

"She knows that he was having an affair, and when we met for lunch the other day, she insinuated that the other woman looked a lot like me."

"What? And your crazy ass took a job working for her?!"

"Royce, I'm desperate."

"No, you're crazy; if you were desperate, you would have gotten some money from Brian, and took your ass to an abortion clinic to end this madness."

"It's not that simple."

"The hell it ain't!" he screamed.

"Puh-lease...." I continued in the same monotone voice.

"Please, my ass! With friends like you, who needs enemies?" He pointed his index finger at me.

"Royce, I thought you would be on my side."

"This isn't about taking sides, Nikole, it's about doing the right thing," He took a moment to calm down and think. "You're on your own with the Brian situation. Hell, I've got problems of my own to worry about, but I'll see what I can do about helping you move."

"Let me go and take a shower so we can get ready for work."

"You do that, and I am going to go in here and try to fix us something to eat. I need to calm my damn nerves." Royce stood up, and with his hand on his hip, he turned in the direction of my kitchen, but I shot him a dirty glance.

"Royce, do you really think I have anything to eat in there? I just told you I'm flat broke and about to be homeless," It was my turn to put my hand on my hip, matching his stance.

"Damn, girl! You don't have shit to eat, either. Get dressed, Nikole, so I can take you to IHOP before you make me cuss you out for real!"

Just as I was about to punch him in his arm, my cell phone started to ring.

"Saved by the ring," he grinned.

"Hello?" I answered in my sexiest voice.

"Bitch, don't think I forgot."

"Bye, Mercedes."

"Keep fucking around with Terrance, and see what's going to happen."

Click.

"I take it that was the P class Mercedes?" Royce asked.

"What in the hell is a P class?"

"Hello … !? Psycho."

Chapter 13

*F*irst we swung by Royce's house so that he could freshen up before we got our grub on at IHOP. Then we headed to the office to put in another full day of selling sex in the city. Royce was pumping Omarion's latest CD, while we hustled to add the finishing touches for the main event. I swear I've never worked so hard in my entire life. Midway through the afternoon I had pulled my hair back into a ponytail and was rolling my neck, trying to work out the kinks.

"Girl, did you get in touch with the midget?"

"I'm still trying. Tell me again why we are hiring a little person?" I naïvely asked Royce.

"The theme is Fantasy Island. You remember the show that used to come on TV with Mr. Roarke and what's his name?"

"Tattoo."

"Yes…Well, I'm going to be Mr. Roarke, and I need a midget to be my sidekick for the night."

"I've heard it all." Nobody but Royce could have come up with an idea like that.

"Did the female strippers call back yet?"

"Black China and Night Queen confirmed."

"Okay, what about the outfits for the female demonstrators?"

I pointed to the box that was sitting next to his feet. "They came in today. Is Bebe really serious about having them wear boy shorts and these ill-fitted tees?" I held one up to my chest while wiggling my nose in dissatisfaction. "What exactly will they be doing, again?"

"Yes, Nikole, the demonstrators, as you like to refer to them, are going to walk around the party with the various products on trays and allow the customers to touch them and see how they work. Think department store cosmetics section." He smiled, and then frowned, "The look on your face says that you don't approve." Royce batted his eyelashes. "Well, do tell, what would you prefer to see them in?"

"I think the shorts are cool, but tank tops would be better." I paused while my idea settled in with Royce. "Cut low in the front to reveal just the right amount of cleavage and hugging all the right curves." I cupped my breasts to get my point across. "More flesh is exposed, which is always a turn on for men and some women, if you know what I mean."

"I see you're starting to get the hang of things." He smiled. "And where are we going to get these shirts in, oh…. a few days?"

"You let me worry about that." I winked. I had to admit that I was starting to get comfortable in my new environment. I also liked the idea of having people ask me my opinions and actually using my suggestions.

"I have got to see this, but if you think you can handle it, you have my blessings."

"This party sounds like it is going to be all that." I placed the shirt back inside of the box.

"Honey, you ain't seen nothing until you check out Zulu and Tight End, the male strippers. *Sweet mother of Jesus!*" He fanned himself.

"Don't start testifying up in here," I laughed.

"Girl, sexy is an understatement, do you hear me? Those two should be outlawed."

"Damn."

"And their bulges are the real thing, not stuffing," he whispered, as if we were secretly planning to commit an unlawful act.

"And how would you know that, Royce?" I looked at him out of the corner of my eyes.

"I did their interviews." He winked, before swishing off.

The line to the office started to ring, and after the fourth one, I decided to play secretary since ours was missing in action again.

"Thank you for calling Erotic Fantasies. This is Nikole speaking."

"Hi, Nikole, this is Melanie."

"Who?"

"Melanie, from Financial Freedom."

Damn, it was the bill collector who had called me a few days ago. "Oh, I'm sorry she's on the phone with a customer. Would you like her voice mail?"

"No, Nikole, I don't want your voice mail. What I do want is to know when can we expect a payment on your outstanding Master Card account that has been placed with our company for collection?" *Damnit, I was busted.*

"Look, I just started working, and I haven't received my first paycheck."

"Why don't you take out a personal loan to pay us back?"

"Obviously, you haven't checked my credit report lately."

"Well, this matter needs to be handled immediately.

"Like everything else in my life," I mumbled. "Look, give me your address, and when I get paid I'll send you something."

"We can take a post-dated check over the telephone."

"I don't have a checking account," I lied. "Look, can you hold on for a minute?"

I pressed the mute button and counted to ten before going back to the persistent caller. When I returned to the line, we agreed on a set amount and after I pretended to jot down their address and repeated it back to Melanie, I ended the call only for the phone to ring again.

"Royce," I yelled towards his office door, which was only a few feet away from my cubicle. "Where in the hell is the receptionist from the temp agency?"

"Who knows…?" he yelled back.

Sighing, I answered the phone again.

"I was hoping you would answer." It was Jackson.

"Oh, really," I leaned back in my chair, twisting the cord happily around my finger. I couldn't suppress the smile that took over my face. This was just what I needed right now to calm my nerves.

I could hear him smiling through the telephone, too. "So, do you get a lunch break?"

"I sure do."

"Okay, I'm on my way to pick you up. Hope you like Chinese."

I wanted to scream, but instead, I remained cool.

"Well, let me wrap up a few things, and I'll be ready. Say twenty minutes?"

"That's perfect."

I hung up the telephone only to hear Boy Wonder's voice coming from the office sound system.

"Hold up, everybody, I've got the boss man in the studio with me. What's up, man?"

"What's up, Wonder? Say man, I need you to play this next cut for this special lady that I'm about to go chill with." I nearly fell out of my seat when I heard Jackson's voice on the radio dedicating a song to me.

"Yo, for you, man, anything…"

The volume on the system went up a notch and I heard *Bonnie & Clyde* coming through the speakers. I shook my head and smiled. Jackson was definitely full of surprises. As I turned around I found Royce doing a great Beyonce booty dance imitation in his office.

Chapter 14

*E*xactly twenty minutes later, Jackson entered the lobby with a dozen pink roses. Karizma, the ghetto secretary who was on loan from the temp agency, had finally arrived. Now she had apparently decided to earn her paycheck by blowing up my phone.

"Girl, there is a fine brother out here who wants to see you," she stated, while chewing on a piece of gum as if her life depended on it. "And if I was you... *hmmm,* all I can say is you'd better hurry up, *girrrl.*" Her Ebonics were killing me, but over all, she seemed like a cool person. I just wished she'd learn some professionalism, starting with getting to work on time. Because of her tardiness I had to deal with a pushy bill collector and lie as if there was no tomorrow.

Grabbing my vintage Louis Vuitton Speedy bag, I checked my appearance for the fifth time before running to the lobby. Deciding to wear a sweat suit, minus an undershirt, because of the elastic waist for my growing waistline, I hoped that I wasn't under dressed for the occasion. As a safety measure, I inched the zipper down on my top to reveal a hint of my B-cup girlfriends. God bless the person who invented the push up bra.

As I entered the lobby, before me stood a blessing from above. I smiled as I took in the beautiful vision of Jackson.

He was dressed from head to toe in authentic Polo gear. I took in a deep breath. Even his cologne was a Ralph Lauren fragrance. His look screamed '*classy*' and with me on his arm, the package was now complete. He had planned on taking me to eat at P.F. Changs, and since I wasn't paying, *hey*...

We entered the contemporary Asian restaurant, and I immediately compared it to the place were Bebe and I had eaten lunch last week. To say that it was Asian, it really lacked the traditional oriental theme. Everything looked Americanized, which kind of disappointed me. As I surveyed the large room, I felt Jackson's arm gently wrap around my waist. I instantly began to smile as I realized that this was the first I had been out in public with a man who wasn't ducking and dodging because he was married.

"Wow, this is nice." I mumbled.

"It's alright. I actually prefer the restaurant were I first saw you." He looked at me tenderly and squeezed my waist to emphasize his statement.

Romantic... I could tell that I was going to really enjoy his company from the easy way that he moved and from the gentle way that he was caressing my back, as we were lead to our table.

"Did I thank you for the flowers and the dedication?"

"Yes, twice." Before he arrived for our date, the floral shop in our office complex came over with a dozen yellow roses, courtesy of Jackson. The fact that he had brought the additional bouquet of pink roses had been the icing on the cake.

"Sorry."

"Don't be. It was my pleasure. Would you like for me to order lunch for you?"

Taken aback, I didn't know what to say. *Okay, so the guy was Mr. Perfect.* Terrance would have started complaining about me taking too long and not knowing what I wanted, and Brian never would have taken me out in public to begin with.

"The orange peel shrimp is good."

"You're running this show." *This was impossible. How could he have known that I love shrimp?* I lowered my eyes to the menu, checking out the description of this shrimp dish. From the looks of things, he was right; it sounded delicious.

After placing our order and sipping on water spiked with lemon, our conversation steered towards relationships.

"So, have you ever been married?"

"Almost," he frowned.

"What happened?"

"I normally don't talk about this…" he sighed, before continuing. "My girlfriend was pregnant so I called myself doing the right thing, and asked her to marry me. On the day of our wedding while waiting in the pastors' office, I noticed that my best man was all tense. He finally told me that he couldn't go through with it. I was confused, because he wasn't the one getting married. His conscience got the best of him, and he came forward and confessed that they had been messing around. The baby she was carrying was actually his." A hollow chuckle escaped from his lips, but the look in his eyes told me that the experience had hurt him deeply. "It was some Jerry Springer shit," he continued.

"I'm sorry to hear that."

"Yeah. So, tell me about you, Nikole."

"Well, you already know about my school situation and that I organize Fun Parties for a living. Let's see… I have a son, Omar. He's two." I smiled. "But his daddy," I shook my head, "is trifling."

"Whoa! Take it easy on the brother. He can't be that bad." He held up his hands in self-defense, supposedly on the behalf of all Black men.

"The hell he can't be." I rolled my neck.

"So, what's up? Are you guys still together?"

"What do you think?"

"Calm down. I'm asking you, baby."

"I had to drag him into court and force his butt to take a DNA test before he would fork over a dime."

"But you didn't answer my question. Are you guys still kicking it?"

"What makes you think that we are?"

"Well, I never said that I thought you guys were, but your body language suggests that you still care about the dude. Hell, he is your baby's daddy. That makes him family."

"How in the hell does that make us related?" I began to regret bringing up my ex on my first official date with this terrific guy. *Damn, I was going to run the man off.*

"Because you have a son together."

"Well, yeah, we kinda have this on again, off again relationship." I looked away. *Me and my big mouth. Why'd I have to go and say that?* He's probably calling me a ho. But when I looked back up, Jackson was still wearing the same sincere expression. I was glad that I'd left out the part about Terrance being married and my being pregnant. He didn't need to know that much about me, at least not yet.

"Well, Nikole, at least you were honest, and I can respect that." He reached out and took my hand in his. "I'm not trying to change your feelings for what's-his-name, but if you continue to hang out with me, hopefully in the end, you'll realize that your son and I are all the men that you need in your life." I had to be dreaming.

I smiled because this brother was full of potential compared to Brian and Terrance, but only time would tell if he was the real deal.

"Most guys don't know when they have a good thing, and they just mess it up by trying to hang out with the fellas or worse, they cheat on their women. That's not me, that's not what I'm about."

"Well, Jackson, I'll keep that in mind." I smiled, while stirring sugar into my newly arrived ice tea.

"So, is what's-his-name helping you out with Omar?"

"His name is Terrance. It's not like I sweat him for child support or to spend time with our son."

"Why not? Isn't his name on the birth certificate too? Sometimes you've got to hold people accountable. If you keep letting them hold you down, then they will."

"Sounds like you missed your calling to be a therapist."

"Naw, I'll leave that up to the professionals like you. I'm happy doing my thing."

"Being a DJ?"

"That, and being with you."

Chapter 15

*A*t this point I was simply trying to maintain my cool and not get my hopes up, because I knew from experience that some men were all talk and no action. I allowed myself to be happy because I knew that it didn't matter. I was falling for him.

As I began to bask in my glory, some hoochie walked up to our table, with her cleavage hanging all out. She had the nerve to ask him for an autograph, completely ignoring me. I eyed her suspiciously as she dipped at the waist, allowing Jackson a full view of her tattooed breast. I cleared my throat, but before I had a chance to say anything, Jackson stepped up to the plate.

"Sorry, sweetheart, but can't you see that I'm out with my lady this afternoon?" He turned his attention back to me, but directed his last remark towards her, "You understand."

All eyes were on me, and I was loving every minute of it. I wanted to laugh in her face, but I just kept my grin on while Hoochie Mama sucked on her teeth and mumbled that he wasn't all that anyway. She trotted back to the horse stable to return the hair that she was wearing, which, might I add, was two shades lighter than her natural hair. Then it hit me! *Did he just call me his lady?* He wasn't wasting any time in marking his territory. I was impressed, but my conscience wouldn't allow me to forget about my sorry excuse of a relationship with Terrance and my scandalous affair with Brian. Shame overwhelmed me. Wasn't I just as bad as the uncaring tramp that had just left our table? Hadn't I ignored the feelings of both Bebe and Mercedes for the sake of having a man, even if he was their man?

"Jackson, I am really feeling you, but I think we should take our time and get to know each other before we rush into anything."

"It's on you, Nikole. I know what I want, and I am willing to play the getting-to-know-you game, or whatever else you want to do."

"You sure are confident."

"How do you think I've gotten this far in life? That's the difference between me and the other guys that you've been hanging out with. I don't just sit back and dream; I devise a master plan, then go out and work my ass off to get what I want. And I want you."

I desperately wanted to believe him so as we continued to talk I took in everything that he was saying. The guy was sharp. He was right; he knew exactly what he wanted out of life: a nurturing relationship, a promising career, you name it and he had it figured out. He talked about his five-year plan which included owning the largest broadcasting network in the country, rental property, a mansion in the country club, and a beautiful wife and kids to share it all with.

His eyes sparkled as he talked about his dreams, and the intensity of his stare let me know that he was dead serious about including me in his plans. This man didn't see me as a one night stand. Again, I was flattered, but I started to feel a little intimidated too.

Come on, any person in their right mind would be scared as hell, especially when they didn't have their stuff together. Honestly, I didn't have a damn thing to offer this guy except some drama.

"A penny for your thoughts."

"Oh, I'm fine." I smiled, half-heartedly.

"I know that, but what's on your mind? You were deep into your thoughts a few seconds ago."

"One day I'll have to fill you in."

"I've been rude rambling on about myself," He leaned across the table and touched my cheek. "Tell me about your plans for the future. What are you going to do since you're not in school?"

"I was hoping you wouldn't ask me that question," I nervously moved my face away, feeling dejected. "To be honest, I don't know what I am going to do, but being employed by my best friend is not going to be an option for too much longer. I am just not comfortable selling vibrating dicks on a key chain, if you know what I mean." I attempted to smile through my resentment. "I tried drawing unemployment, right before Bebe offered me this job, but the entire process was just too humiliating." I began to play with my hands. "Sometimes it feels like my world is just falling apart." I looked up to meet the intensity of his warm eyes again.

"So what are you going to do? Are you going to sit around and wait for someone to give you a job, or venture out and create your own opportunities?"

"Royce said the same thing."

"Great minds think alike, and he's right. Those people are flat out telling you that they aren't going to give you anything."

"I guess you are right."

He shook his head, "Don't guess, Nikole. You need to know it."

"I just don't want to rush into anything and then be sorry later."

"Are we still talking about careers, or have we switched back to relationships?" His eyebrow arched slightly.

"You tell me."

His smile was naughty as he avoided my question skillfully, "So, are you ready to head out?"

"I'm riding with you."

Jackson signaled for the waitress. After reviewing the bill, I noticed that he pulled out a black American Express card. His people must have a little cheese, because I couldn't imagine some one living on a DJ's salary having one of those babies. My bourgie instincts kicked in. Only the elite carried those around. A jolt of anger coursed through my veins. If it weren't for Daddy Dearest I'd still be flexing with my card. As I rose from my chair, Jackson came around, slid it from underneath me, and took my hand. Once I was on my feet, he didn't let go.

"Do you mind?"

"What?" I smiled.

"If I hold your hand?"

"No, not at all," A warm, comforting feeling took over my body as he tightened his grip around my small fingers, and I secretly hoped that he would never let go.

The weather had changed drastically since the beginning of our lunch date, which is typical in south Louisiana. The day had transformed from bright sunshine to a freaking monsoon, and the rain had started to pour down.

"Wait here." Jackson instructed me.

As I waited for him to pull his Escalade around, I noticed a familiar face walking up to the restaurant. We locked eyes, and my blood began to boil. *Damn, it was Terrance.* I just knew that my eyes were deceiving me, because this Negro had the nerve to have his arm draped around some Asian supermodel looking chick. I was in a good mood, and I didn't want him to spoil it, so instead of waiting for Jackson, I raced out to his SUV and hopped in.

"Damn girl, I was coming to get you."

"A little rain won't hurt," I huffed.

As Jackson eased out of the parking lot, I looked back. Jealousy seeped through my veins, but I brushed that shit off when my eyes traveled in Terrance's direction. Suddenly, I was livid. This bastard had gotten skimpy with the funds, and now I knew why. He had the nerve to be pushing a white Range Rover, sitting on thirty-two inch rims, and sporting a temporary license tag! Now you know I was mad as hell, but I also felt played. That beat up Cutlass was just a front. He had been poor mouthing to me, but out in public he was acting like a playa. Not to mention, *who in the hell was that on his arm?!*

This was the icing on the cake; I had seen enough. Now he was going to see my ass in court. If he knew like I did, child support would not be missing him. I turned back to look at Jackson, who was jamming to *Put 'Em In Their Place* by Mobb Deep, and instantly it became my theme song.

"You alright?"

"Yeah," I managed to squeak, dislodging the lump that was caught in my throat.

Jackson reached over and squeezed my thigh. I was glad that he had not picked up on my mood change.

As I sat there contemplating my situation, being in the company of a decent guy was helping me to realize what I had been missing in a relationship - hell, in a man. But the vibrating of my phone halted my thoughts. As I reached inside of my purse, the number flashing on the screen signaled that it was Terrance calling from his cell phone. *Naw, don't call me now,* I grimaced, and pressed the ignore button.

Chapter 16

I couldn't wait to get back to the office to tell Royce about my date. When I arrived, he was in a heated discussion on the telephone with Charles, so instead, I made my way back to my gray cubicle. I was greeted by another floral arrangement, but unlike the ones I had received from Jackson, that were taking there designated place next to my computer screen so that I could stare at them during the day, this one looked so out of place sitting in the center of my desk.

Curious, I pulled out the attached card and read, *"With all my love, Terrance."* I know my eyes must have been deceiving me. I stared at the card in disbelief. He must have ordered them right after I refused to answer his call. He could be nice when he wanted to, but I knew what this was about. I couldn't believe the nerve of this fool. The minute he thinks there is another man in my life, he wants to start playing me close, but if my memory serves me right, just the other day I was nothing more than his baby's mama getting on his nerve about child support.

As I settled into my antiquated, wooden, executive chair, I tossed the card into the trash can before noticing that the red message light was blinking on my phone. I had four messages. One was from Budget about their rental car.

"Stalkers," I muttered under my breath.

The perky voice urged that I return their car immediately before her manager decided on a legal course of action.

"All of this for a rental car?" I really needed to get my car fixed, but with all of the other stuff that was going on in my life, I was barely finding time to think these days, let alone worry about a stupid vehicle. The next message was from my mother telling me that I needed to stop by and visit Omar.

"Okay, but I just saw him a few days ago," I thought to myself. She could be so annoying. But I did need to spend some time with him. Maybe I would swing by there after work if I got out of here before his bedtime tonight.

The third message was from Mercedes.

"You better watch your back."

I quickly pressed the number seven and erased her irritating voice from my life. I wondered if she harassed Miss Exotic from the restaurant like this.

The last voice that I heard was Brian, asking me if I had taken care of that issue. Holding the receiver in my hand, I contemplated calling him back and cussing him out since he hadn't made any monetary donations towards our issue, but the sound of Terrance's voice interrupted my thoughts.

"What's up, Nikole?" His eyes scanned my work area, and he smiled when they landed on the flowers that he had sent earlier. He was so self-absorbed that I know he didn't even take any notice of the other bouquets. "I see you got them."

"What do you want?" I hung up the receiver and folded my arms across my chest with the meanest look that I could muster consuming my face.

He stepped into the cubicle.

"What, a brother can't get some love?" His arms extended out as he waited for me to greet him.

"Like I said…what do you want?" I didn't move from my seat.

Seeing that I was pissed off, he leaned over my desk and tried to kiss me, but I turned my head.

"So it's like that?"

"It sure is."

"Since you acting all funny, where's my son?"

"Where else? At my parents' house."

"Why you always ditching my kid?"

"First of all, I'm at work, Negro. Secondly, I don't see you trying to spend any time with him, so leave me the hell alone."

"Whatever, Nikole."

"So, where have you been, all dressed up?" I glared at him, daring him to lie. Instead he just smirked at me and took a seat.

"You didn't answer me?" I began to sound irate.

"You already know the answer," he winked, "and I know you ain't over there acting mad and shit."

"Really," I huffed, with my arms still crossed.

"And who was ole boy?"

"You're worried about the wrong damn thing, Terrance." I was still trying to act mad, but just looking at him was making me weaker by the minute.

"Come here." He patted his thigh. Stupidly, I dropped my guard and rounded my desk, where I promptly took a seat in his lap.

"Why you got your lip poked out? What's wrong with you?" He gently touched my lip.

"Look, I know we're not married, but don't disrespect me." I tried to regain some semblance of dignity.

"That goes both ways, Nikole." He planted a soft kiss on my cheek as his hand began to creep up the front of my jacket. "Let me make it up to you." He nibbled on my ear.

"I'm at work, Terrance," I tried to brush his hand away, but he refused to stop. As he fondled my nipples I heard my lust filled voice betraying me. "I need some money, baby."

"How about this, instead," He dangled a diamond tennis bracelet before my eyes. Don't ask me what happened next. I must have snapped, because before I knew it, my lustful feelings had packed up and took a leave of absence, and I was going off on Terrance.

I pushed his arm away from me. "Shit, for the price of this you could have paid my damn rent! Better yet, the electric bill that I just forked over four hundred dollars to have my shit turned back on!" My voice went up a few octaves, but Terrance ignored my complaining as he attempted to secure the bracelet on my wrist. Like a dummy, I continued to protest.

"Damn, Nikole, can you just shut the fuck up?" he snapped back.

I twisted my body around so that I could face him. "I don't need another piece of jewelry, Terrance. What I need is some money to pay my damn bills and to help take care of our son."

"I bust my ass trying to make you happy. Buying you designer shit and flying your ass all over the world, but you're never happy. No, all you fuckin' do is complain."

"You know what?!" I snatched the bracelet off of my arm, "I don't need shit from you!" I threw the trinket in his face.

"Bitch…"

In a state of shock, I found myself sitting dumbfounded on the floor, holding the side of my face. Sure he had tried to choke the shit out of me a few times, and of course there was the incident of him abandoning me that night. Let's also not forget the condescending way he tended to speak to me, but this hitting and pushing was starting to get out of hand.

"Get out!" I heard Royce yelling at the top of his lungs. "Get the hell out of here before I call the damn police!" I didn't realize that Royce was standing there, but at that moment I didn't care. I knew the extent of Terrance's wrath, and I just wanted him to get far away from me.

"You ain't nothing but a jump off, Nikole," he smirked.

"Well, we're going to do more than jump off in this mutha if you stay here one minute longer," I watched as Royce reached inside of his pocket and pulled out his trusty switch blade.

"Fucking sissy."

"And this sissy will cut your ass, just try me." Royce narrowed his eyes as he flipped open the blade.

I glared at Terrance through hate filled, teary eyes, "Just leave, Terrance!"

"Don't you raise your voice at me, Nikole."

"Uh, Terrance, We all know that you rode the short school bus to school, so let me say this so that your special ass will understand. You've worn out your welcome. If you don't start walking towards the front door, the coroner's office is going to have to put your jigsaw puzzle ass back together." Royce threatened evenly.

Glaring at me, Terrance snatched the bracelet off of the floor and stormed out of the office.

"Thank you, Royce."

"Don't think this shit is over with…" He reached out his hand to help me get up from the floor, "Next time you may not be so lucky, Nikole." After Royce made sure that I was safe, he headed for the employee lounge, leaving me to my thoughts.

I sat at my desk stewing in humiliation and contemplating my next move, when I heard voices coming from Bebe's office.

"Fuck you, Brian!"

"This is bullshit, Bebe, and you know it."

What in the hell was he doing here?! I wanted to be nosey and put my ear to the door, but Bebe was still my boss and unfortunately, I still needed this job. So, I decided to give them a hint that someone else was within hearing range by turning on the stereo system and pretending that I was working.

As I sorted through all of the stuff that was scattered across my desk searching for something official looking to hold in my hands, I tossed aside a pair of edible panties and grabbed a merchandise invoice as Bebe's office door swung open. To my surprise, out walked my red-faced friend and the source of my present problem.

Dressed in a navy Armani suit, Brian usually looked fabulous, but for some reason he looked used-the-hell-up today. I couldn't help but to stare. I felt sorry for him. Then I noticed that Bebe was watching me, watching him. I diverted my eyes to a piece of lint I had discovered on my jogging suit. I thought about my situation, our situation, and how he had abandoned me. My feelings shifted from pity to anger.

"Nikole, how are things going?" He stepped towards my desk, with his back facing Bebe. I stood to give him a hug.

"What's up, Brian?" We hugged briefly, and then he took a small step back.

"Girl, you're still looking good." He touched my stomach lightly, as he stared into my eyes with a questioning look.

Looking over his shoulder I felt the heat from Bebe's eyes penetrating through his back. Embarrassed, I flashed a quick smile to mask my discomfort.

"Thanks I do what I can."

"And look at you...! Is that a new suit?" My hand grazed the top of his right bicep, lingering there a second too long. I wanted to slap the hell out of him, but I refrained. My time would come.

Bebe had a quizzical look on her tear-stained face. She had been married to this man since they were nineteen years old. She had been my friend forever. She knew us both very well. I'm quite sure that she knew something wasn't right.

"So, has Bebe been keeping you busy?" He turned and flashed his wife a tense, ultra white smile.

I used the opportunity to step back from him, suspended my hand in mid-air above my desk, ala the models from that television game show, *The Price is Right*. I stated, "The sight of my desk should answer that question for you."

The room became awkwardly quiet for a second.

"Well, I've got to go." With a serious expression weighing down his face, he turned towards Bebe. "I'll send the paperwork over on Monday."

"Nikole, it was good to see you again." He forced a smile, as he turned to leave.

When I thought he was gone, I turned to my friend. "What's going on with you two?" I asked more to be nosey verses being a concerned friend.

"He wants a divorce."

"So, why are you crying? I thought that was what you wanted."

"Yeah… no…hell, I don't know!" she sniffled. "Girl, Brian is my soul mate. We belong together. I could never be happy without him in my life."

"I guess." I shrugged my shoulders. *Hell, what was I supposed to say?* Personally, I thought she sounded a little desperate.

"He's just confused right now, but I'm not worried. He'll come around."

"You think so?"

That's when she snapped. "Fuck Brian! He didn't have shit when I met his sorry ass, and he won't have shit if he tries to divorce me. He's forgotten who worked two jobs so he could go to law school full-time. I made him the man that he's become, and I'll be damned if another bitch is going to stop me from getting what's rightfully *mine*."

You're right about that, girlfriend. If it wasn't for you pushing him to be perfect, and you, pretending to be perfect, then maybe he would stay at home versus running into the arms of every available woman that shows him the time of day. Maybe if you'd stop putting so much time into this sex factory and worked on your damn marriage, your best friend wouldn't be standing here carrying your husband's baby.

Out loud, I asked her, "Bebe, are you positive he's having an affair?"

"Pictures don't lie." She rubbed her temples.
Fuck! I thought to myself.

"Do you need anything?" I folded my arms across my chest, as I continued to play the dutiful friend.

Her eyes were filled with tears, but not one fell from her eyes. "Can you imagine how I'm feeling? When we took those vows we made a promise before God that we would stay together until death do us part, not until Brian decided to have an affair and get his mistress pregnant knowing that his wife desperately wants kids of her own."

"I'm sorry, Bebe." I really felt bad now. The thought never crossed my mind that Bebe may have been trying to conceive.

"Why, it's not like he was screwing you!" Her reply was sarcastic, as she looked at me all crazy.

My hormones were all over the place, and just like that I went from feeling guilty to suppressing the urge to punch her in her throat. I decided to keep my damn mouth closed, and I shoved my hands in the front pockets of my jacket before I did something that I might regret.

"Hey… I'm fine." She reached out and gave me a hug. "I'm just stressed about this party and having everything go according to my plans, in addition to this fiasco with Brian." Her fingers had returned to her temples and as they moved faster, her eyes kept going up and down. "I just need a little time to get myself together. Figure out some things."

"Everything is going to turn out fine." I stood there secretly wanting her to leave. "Get out of here. This stuff can wait until tomorrow." I used my words to comfort her. Encourage her to do my will.

Bebe's smile was stiff, but her posture was beginning to loosen up. She returned to her office to gather her things and then she made a mad dash for the door. "You got everything under control?"

"Of course."

The minute I heard the buzzer for the front door, I raced towards her office. It was time to find out if my hunch about the identity of the woman who had sent that porn magazine to Mercedes was correct.

Chapter 17

*A*s soon as my ass hit the soft leather of her executive
chair, my eyes scanned Bebe's luxurious office. Done in
rich Earth tones; it was a place of calmness, peace and
tranquility. The sound of running water floated through her
surround sound speakers and the delicious sent of a vanilla
bean candle still burned on her desk. Hopefully I would find
some peace of my own here tonight. Maybe her office
would help to end the nagging feeling that was growing in
the pit of my stomach. As I continued to take in the
expensive furnishings and exquisite Black art, my eyes
landed on the day planner that Bebe had left behind.
Furiously, I began to thumb through it, staring at the
handwriting in disbelief. As I was attempting to return it to
her desk, a lipstick imprinted sticky note slipped out and
floated lazily towards the floor. I reached down and picked
up the yellow piece of paper, cursing under my breath.
    "That bitch."
    With the truth staring me in my face, there wasn't a damn
thing that I could do except try and figure out why she would
purposefully send Mercedes after me. That nagging feeling
had returned to my stomach. She knew about us.
After making sure everything was in place, I closed the door
to her office and went to track down Royce in the break
room. As soon as I walked in, I headed straight to the soda
machine. I know I wasn't supposed to have products with

caffeine in them, but I desperately needed a Coke to settle my nerves.

"Hey, what are you doing?" Royce was stretched out on the worn out sofa, which was exactly how he looked. "When are you going to stop letting Terrance hit on you?" He responded, pointedly, never taking his eyes off of the television screen.

"Royce, do we have to talk about him?"

"Somebody needs to talk to you before you end up in the hospital or worse."

"You just don't understand. He just gets a little upset sometimes."

"Upset…?" He propped himself up on one arm and stared at me in disbelief. "That man is *crazy*! Hell, he's married to Mercedes, and you know that nobody in their right mind would be legally attached to her."

I just shook my head and smiled.

"Correct me if I'm wrong, but wasn't that the same Mercedes who ran out on the basketball court in Italy when her husband got into a fight with a player from the opposing team, kicking the poor guy in the knee, and ending his promising basketball career? And didn't she just come onto your job and threaten you, Nikole?" See, that's what I loved about my dear friend, he was so insightful.

"Okay… and?" I shrugged my shoulders.

"You can keep being a fool, but I know Mercedes ain't over there off of Coursey Boulevard in her little gated community letting Terrance hit on her."

I just stared at Royce, because I really didn't have an answer.

"Anyway, you asked me what I was doing. I'm looking in the classifieds for a car, half-ass watching *The Real Housewives of Atlanta*, and eating some rocky road ice cream." He plopped down on the sofa, again.

Only at Erotic Fantasies, I thought. Sensing that there was something going on with Royce, I decided to pry a little.

"Okay, so what's wrong with you?" I stood over him, sipping on my soda as a look of satisfaction crept across my face in appreciation of the thirst quenching drink.

"Check her out." Royce pointed around me, in the direction of the thirty-two inch television that Bebe used to have at home, before she made Brian go out and buy that giant plasma thing that they probably never watch. "That NeNe is a mess."

"Who?"

"Don't you watch this?" Royce questioned.

"You watch too much television, Royce."

"Honey, how do you think I stay on top of things when it comes to fashion? It's called BET, MTV and anything else that comes on TV." I noticed that he was trying to be upbeat, but in reality he still looked pitiful.

"Royce, sweetie, what's wrong?" I took a seat next to him on the fake leather sofa.

"What makes you think that there is something wrong?"

"Just a hunch."

"It's Charles," he sighed. "We had another argument."

"What happened this time?"

"Underwear."

"Okay, let me brace myself for this one."

Royce rolled his eyes at me before continuing; "I found a pair of men's boxers when I was washing clothes. I am not a boxer kind of guy, so they sure in the hell don't belong to me."

"I'm not following you Royce. You washed the man's dirty underwear and...?"

"You and Terrance are made for each other because you are dumber than a box of rocks, too. Nikole, the undies were for somebody else."

"Charles was fucking around in your crib with another man!?"

"*Praise the Lord!* I think we just had a break through." He raised a hand towards the ceiling.

"Ha, ha. Very funny."

"Yeah, well, you know the Negro denied it until the end," he paused. "I deserve better, Nikole."

Tears began to stream down his face. Honestly, I couldn't take another emotional outburst, but unlike Bebe, I actually did care about Royce.

"You know... I've been through hell and back in just this one lifetime, Nikole."

"I know, Royce." I took his hand in mine. "Life isn't fair."

"And to top it off, my dad has been calling me."

"What did he want?" *Chester, Chester, the child molester.*

"I haven't talked to him, but he's been leaving messages about being ill and wanting to see me."

If losing his mother to cancer when we were in elementary school wasn't bad enough, try being raised by a daddy who happens to like getting his groove on with little boys.

"So, are you going to call him?"

Royce jerked his hand away from me. "Hell no!"

"Royce..."

"I've been fine for the last sixteen years, without him. Why would I want to call him now?" He did have a point, but I just couldn't understand how people could cut their ties with their family off, just like that, regardless of what had taken place between them in the past. But then again, my father didn't molest me.

"Hell, my nerves are so bad, I had to go and see a real therapist."

"You're joking, right?"

"Hell, no."

"Well... what did the therapist say?"

"Some shit about how my attraction to noncommittal men is somehow related to the abuse."

"I can see that..."

"Well, I'm glad you can see what my problem is. So, what's your excuse?" He turned his attention back to the newspaper.

I know he didn't just go there with me! I took a deep breath and tried to be upbeat as we continued our conversation. "Royce, maybe Charles is telling the truth."

"Girl, puh-lease! A fool, I am not."

"Speaking of fools and lies, guess why Terrance was up here earlier?"

"A sparring match? Hell, I don't know."

"Royce!"

"Look Nikole, I don't know, and besides, I thought we were talking about me," he pouted.

I sighed, falling against the plush pillows that adorned the sofa.

"Don't tell me he saw Brian leaving your apartment this morning?"

"What are you talking about?" I played the dumb blonde role, but inside, I found myself cursing.

"Play dumb if you want to, but the walls in your apartment are paper thin."

Flushed, I tried to respond, but found myself stumbling over my words. "I saw him when I was out with Bri... I mean, Jackson this afternoon."

Royce arched his perfectly waxed eyebrow at me. I knew he had heard my slip up, "And what happened?"

"He was with some Korean chick, and check this out," I patted his arm.

"What?" He perked up with excitement.

"He was pushing a Range Rover."

"Get out of here."

"So, why was he over here bootin' up?"

"Cause he is crazy."

"I'm telling you, Nikole..."

"And Royce, tell me why the man sent me some flowers after I busted his ass, then got pissed off when I refused to accept a diamond tennis bracelet from him?"

"No, *you're stupid*. I would have taken that bracelet to the nearest pawn shop." His voice went up an octave as he sat upright. "Now you know what you need to do."

"Yeah. I just didn't want to get the courts involved."

"Girl, please stop feeling sorry for him, because Terrance sure isn't sitting at home trying to figure out how to leave his wife for you. Believe that."

"You're right." Suddenly, I was anxious to change the subject, "So, what's in the paper?"

"Hey, listen to this…" He snatched the classified section open, "A 1968 Mercedes. It needs some work, aka love, and a good home. Mine. Priced to sell at $1,500."

It seems I wasn't the only one with car problems. Royce's car was totaled in an accident almost two years ago. He refuses to say who was at fault, but he drives like a bat out of hell and doesn't like to wear his prescription glasses. I think it's safe to conclude that he may have caused it.

"Why are you trying to buy a car that's older than you are, and one that is named after my worst enemy?"

"Girl, that's a classic! Let's go and take a look at it." He perked up.

"I don't know what men see in these old ass cars and besides, I just got back from lunch. Bebe is going to kill me if I don't get this work completed." I complained.

"Stop whining."

"Why, you do it all of the time?" I teased. "Why don't you try and buy something new, Royce? I mean, really, couldn't you just ask your dad to help you out since he's trying to be a part of your life again?"

"First off, your precious 1990 BMW is also considered a classic, even if it is sitting at the auto repair shop patiently waiting for its owner to pay for a new transmission. Secondly, how in the world do I form my lips to ask my dad for help after what he did to me? I don't know about you, Nikole, but I don't like being around people who hurt me." He took a deep breath. "Okay… I'm getting off of that subject. We were talking about me needing a car. And for your information sweetheart, Bebe is gone for the day. She left right after Brian so we can just tell her, if she even asks, that we were at the party store picking up more decorations."

"But that's lying."

Royce rolled his eyes before acknowledging me. "Don't try and act like you're a saint, and besides, it's really not a lie. That is on our to-do list for today any damn way. We'll just be making a little pit stop."

Ignoring Royce, I checked my cell phone to make sure I had cut it back on and to make sure I hadn't missed any calls.

"Nikole, I didn't want to suggest this at first, but because you're my friend, I think I need to."

"What, Royce?" I looked up to find my friend staring at me with an intensity I had never seen in all the years that we had known each other.

"You need to see a damn shrink too."

"Why would you suggest that?"

"Oh, I don't know. Maybe it has something to do with Terrance leaving you stranded in the middle of nowhere, or me finding him standing over you about to kick your ass at work? Then there's the little issue of you fucking your best friend's husband."

"I could say the same thing about you. You go from one relationship to the next, and if the man makes one little mistake you kick him out of your life." I lashed back.

"Well, at least I've admitted that I have a problem, and I'm getting some professional help. Your ass is still in denial."

"People make mistakes, but they can also change." I softened up. "And I don't need to see a therapist."

Agitated, he asked, "So, you think Terrance is going to wake up one morning and stop beating the hell out of you? Or that Brian is going to up and leave Bebe one day, and you guys are going to live happily ever after? Never mind; don't even answer that."

Chapter 18

*A*s usual, Royce and I didn't stay mad with each other very long, and I ended up taking him to look at his future car. After checking out the 'classic', we headed to Wal-mart to pick up a few items and some how ended up at Sassy Nails.

Brian had been working on my last good nerve most of the afternoon. As my cell phone vibrated across the arm of the pedicure chair, I glanced at the caller ID and noticed that it was him, again. *That was call number fifteen, but who was counting?*

"Hmm, looks like someone is jealous," Royce teased, as he blew on his freshly manicured nails.

"It's Brian, not Terrance."

"Oh, my bad, problem number two." Royce shook his head and began to talk to the manicurist.

Reluctantly, I flipped open my phone.

"Hi."

"Nikole, when are you going to take care of that problem?"

"When you bring me some money." I took the defensive approach.

"Don't play with me."

"Brian, I shouldn't have to ask you to help me take care of this."

"I think you were right, she knows about us."

"Whatever, you're getting off of the subject, which is the problem that we have growing in my belly, and I think you might be right. I didn't give her enough credit, but the girl figured it out."

"How do you know? Did she say anything?" The nervousness rose in his voice. *Oh, now we're concerned.*

"Look, just get me some money, so I can take care of this."

"Where are you?"

"That's not important. Just get me the damn money, so that I can make this go away, and everyone can move on with their lives."

"I'm coming over tonight. So we can talk face to face," he commanded.

"Really? Look, I don't need you to come over to my place to remind me about what I need to do, Brian. Just mail me a money order or better yet, take down my bank account number and deposit the money into my account." He was the last person that I needed to see right now, especially if I was going to go through with this. Seeing him would only make things worse. No, this was the only way to handle this situation, and get myself out of this mess.

"Correction, Nikole. You need me to do more than remind your ass or simply hand you a check. You need me to take you to the clinic my damn self, because that's the only way I can guarantee that this abortion will happen." *See, now why'd he have to go there? I'm the one that's going to have a life sucked out of her, and he's the one bitching!*

"Hell, if you would have handled your business in the first place, we wouldn't be having this stupid ass conversation." I fumed. "I see why Bebe put your ass out."

"And what do you think she'll do to you if she finds out that you slept with me while she and I were still together?

Don't be stupid, Nikole." His voice dominated the line. "I'll see you tonight," he stated, before disconnecting the call.

Pissed, I shoved the phone into my purse and abruptly ended my pedicure. I guess the elderly Vietnamese woman doing my toes overheard the conversation, because in her broken English, she informed me that it wasn't a problem.

"Hell, I guess not. You made me pay for this shit before you even got started." I placed a perfectly manicured nail to my temple. Another headache was in the forecast. I really needed to talk to the doctor about these damn things. I rolled down the pants legs to my warm up suit and slipped on the flimsy flip-flops that the technician had given to me earlier. I was about to leave the hunched back woman a tip, but then I remembered that I had used my Visa card to pay for everything, which, I am sure had just pushed me over my limit.

"And what did lover boy want?" Royce hovered over me as I tried to get myself together.

"This pregnancy to disappear."

"Y'all have issues."

"I can handle Brian."

"Yeah, that's what they all say before they end up in the ER talking about they ran into a 'door'."

"Brian doesn't hit me."

"Naw, he just sexes you down then goes home to your girl. Hey, do you have change for a five? I need to leave this woman a tip." Royce reached the crisp bill over to me.

"No." I pushed my Valentino shades up to shield my eyes from the sun as I grabbed the door handle to leave.

"Damn, never mind, Nikole," Royce handed the manicurist the entire five.

"You come back soon." I heard one of them say, but my mind was clearly on other things as I clicked the remote to unlock the doors to the rental.

We entered the highway, and Royce jabbered away about his problems with Charles. I caught something about how the man might be married.

"Great, just what the world needs, another brotha on the down low," I mumbled to myself.

Chapter 19

*W*ith the relaxing sounds of Tyrese purring from the sound system in my car, I thought about my date with Jackson. Just thinking about those well-defined arms being wrapped around my body sent shivers up my spine. At that moment, my cell phone began to vibrate. I didn't even glance at the ID screen because my instincts told me who it was.

"You miss me?" I giggled, anticipating Jackson's soothing voice on the other line.

"What do you think? What's up?" He didn't disappoint.

"Royce and I just finished being pampered." I glanced at Royce, who was sitting in my passenger's seat admiring his own hands.

"Really?" Jackson sounded amused.

"Really."

"So, can I see how a freshly pampered Nikole looks later on tonight or what?"

"Actually, I have plans for tonight, but maybe we can get together this weekend or early next week."

The line was filled with silence.

"I promise you, it will be worth the wait."

"Umm look, Nikole, I guess I need to be upfront with you about my intentions. I am really feeling you, but I'm not trying to compete with another guy. My time is valuable, and I don't want to be wasting it on a lost cause. So, if you and your ex are trying to work things out, just let me know, okay?"

"Hey, it's not even like that," I tried to sound upbeat, but deep down I was hurt by his statement. He didn't know what I was thinking at that moment, and it sure in the hell wasn't Terrance.

"Call me when you figure out what you want to do."
I already knew what I wanted to do. I didn't need to figure anything else out.

"Hey, what did you have in mind for tonight?"

"I have tickets to a concert."

"The only people in town are…. Oh my goodness!
You've got tickets to see The Wailers! That's impossible.
That concert has been sold out for weeks."

"Perks of the business baby, so what's up?"

"What time should I be ready?"

"I'll be at your place around nine."

"I'll see you then."

Unable to contain my excitement, I hurried towards the daycare center to scoop up Omar, since my mom had refused to keep him for another night.

I turned to Royce, "You're still one of my best friends, right?"

"What do you need me to do, Nikole?" He cut his eyes in my direction.

"Jackson has tickets to see The Wailers, and I need a babysitter."

"Shit, ya'll didn't get me a ticket? What's really going on around here?"

"Please, Royce, I'll owe you one."

"Try two or three, honey."

"I love you, Royce." I sang out to him.

"Yeah, yeah, yeah…"

After we arrived at my place, Royce began to inspect the outfit that I was planning to wear and gave me a few tips about attending a reggae concert. That's what I loved about him the most. He was brutally honest when it came to fashion. He would never let me leave out of the house unless I was looking my very best.

"Now, it's okay to share weed."

"What! Boy, you are crazy."

"Girl, there is going to be so much blazing up in that place that the Fire Marshall might come in and shut that shit down."

"Royce, you are a fool."

"Are you wearing that?" He pointed to my faded jeans and Bob Marley t-shirt.

"What's wrong with my outfit?"

"You need to show the man some flesh. Let him know what you're working with."

"Here…" He reached inside of my closet. "Wear this."

"A halter top?"

"Flesh, darling." He stepped back inside of my closet and pulled out a pair of stilettos.

"You must be crazy, heels at a concert. My feet will be killing me."

"That's the price you'll have to pay if you want to be the baddest looking bitch in the place. Now stop complaining, and put on the damn outfit."

After Royce did my hair and make up, I twirled around in front of the mirror. I had to admit that I was looking fierce. Five minutes later Jackson was ringing my doorbell, and his facial expression let me know that he thought I had it going on too.

Chapter 20

Royce was right, I was high as a kite the minute I stepped foot inside of the building. The cloud of smoke was so thick that I had trouble focusing, but after a few moments my entire body adjusted. It wasn't even necessary for me to light one up because I was soaring from the contact alone. Jackson was the perfect gentleman the entire night, but he did look at me funny when I turned down a Red Stripe beer.

"You can't come to a reggae concert and not drink a Red Stripe, Nikole."

"Try me." I was still having my doubts about an abortion, and I didn't want to take any chances and mess up the baby's health if I did decide to keep it.

One step away from sexing the man down on the dance floor, I allowed the music to take me away from all of my problems as we danced until the wee hours of the morning to all of the classic hits by The Wailers. The members had changed, but the music was still the same after all of these years. To my surprise, my feet weren't killing me after all, and Royce was right, I was the baddest bitch in the joint.

As we exited the Varsity, where the concert was being held, Jackson held my hand. "It's kinda crowded in here, and I wouldn't want you to get lost in the crowd."

All I could do was smile. Yeah, it was a corny excuse to hold my hand, but I was feeling his corniness. It felt so good to be out on the town with a man who was concerned about my well being and not about what was between my legs and not having to worry about some deranged wife or girlfriend lurking in the shadows.

"You hungry?"

"After all of that weed, what do you think?" I laughed.

We took a short walk over to Louise Café, where we settled into a window booth and munched on one of their famous homemade burgers.

"Honestly, I didn't think you would come with me to the concert tonight."

"Why not?"

"You don't seem like a reggae kind of girl."

"Well, there are a lot of things that you don't know about me." I plopped a tater tot into my mouth.

"But I'm willing to learn if you'll teach me," he grinned.

After we finished dining, we returned to Jackson's home for a nightcap. When we turned into the entrance of River Place Condominiums, an elaborate residential complex that overlooked the Mississippi River in downtown Baton Rouge, my mouth dropped to the floor.

To my amazement, I was greeted by a candlelit condo, and in the background Eric Benet was singing about wanting to be loved. Following his lead, I removed my shoes at the front door entrance.

"How did you pull this off?" I asked as I surveyed his vast living quarters.

"Margie, my housekeeper."

"You have a housekeeper?"

"Yeah. Would you like something to drink? I have wine, beer, juice and bottled water."

"Bottled water is fine."

While he went to get me something to drink, I took the liberty of roaming around his all white living room. I admired the enormous tropical fish tank, the numerous awards for his work in the field of broadcasting, and his large collection of books. On his shelf were titles such as *The Mis-Education of the Negro, What They Forgot to Teach You in History Class,* and *The Isis Papers,* just to name a few. Pictures of him with an older couple also caught my eye. Jackson and the lady with the million-dollar smile could easily pass for fraternal twins, so I concluded that those people must be his parents.

"I see you've met the family." The sound of his voice filled the air. I nodded then looked around at the numerous candles that were lighting up the room.

"So, do you always come home to a candlelit house at night?"

"Nope."

"So, what's the special occasion?"

"Not what, who," He smiled as he handed me a chilled bottle of sparkling water. "If they're bothering you, I can blow them out."

"No, no…they're nice. Thank you."

"Come on, let's have a seat."

Jackson took my hand and led me towards the white leather sofa, where he focused all of his attention on me. "Give me your feet."

Without a second thought, I reclined on the soft leather and swung my feet into his lap. After a few seconds I felt the gentle touch of his hands kneading my soles.

"You've got a lot of pent up tension."

"If only you knew."

"Relax; let me take care of you." *Lord, those words were music to my ears.* No man had ever said those things to me!

Settling deeper into the comfort of his sofa, I allowed myself to let go. His touch was exhilarating, and it took all of my willpower not to pull him on top of me.

"How does that feel?"

"Too good," I moaned

"Sit on my lap," his voice dropped to a sexy whisper.

Without any questions I straddled his lap as Jackson lifted my shirt and his hands glided and caressed the muscles in my back. I jumped when he touched a sore spot.

"You okay?"

"Yeah, I just need to hang out with you more often."

"Is that a promise?" He kissed the tip of my nose.

"You'd better believe it,"

I slid my tongue inside of his mouth, enjoying the warmth that was hidden there. Jackson hands moved from my back to my breasts, and I felt my panties getting moist as my nipples began to harden from the excitement.

Soon, my hands decided to do some exploring of their own as I fumbled with his belt buckle, trying to reach that growing bulge that was about to burst out of his jeans. As I reached inside of his pants, I took in a deep breath. The brother was definitely packing in all of the right places. I stroked his male ego, as his fingers explored the source of my increasing wetness. The passion between us was so intense that I thought I was having a heat stroke.

"Damn."

"What, baby?"

"Nothing. Just enjoying the moment."

"If you let me, I'll make sure you have a lot of moments like this," He kissed me hard before his hands untied my halter top, and he began to plant warm kisses on my breasts. I grabbed his head with my free hand, while my other hand continued to stroke his erection. Soon our clothes were lying haphazardly on the floor as Jackson's hands continued to explore every inch of my body.

"Give me a second." Jackson moved from the sofa to the kitchen, returning seconds later with an ice cube. Smiling mischievously, he demanded that I lie on my back. I watched as he inserted the ice cube into his mouth and began to retrace the path that his hands had taken earlier. I arched my back, my body demanding more. With the ice cube still in his mouth Jackson nestled his face at the center of my very being, making my body scream with desire.

Just as things started to really heat up, my cell phone began to vibrate. A worried look crossed Jackson's face, but I knew it was only Royce, calling to see why I hadn't made it home.

When we returned to my place, we found Royce and Omar passed out on the sofa, surrounded by packing boxes and *Cat in the Hat* watching them from the television.

"I guess I'd better be going since little man is going to be home tonight. I wouldn't want him to wake up in the morning and get the wrong impression." He was thinking about the well being of my child. *Jackson was definitely a keeper!*

Surprisingly, we hadn't gone all the way, and I was still hot with desire. I really didn't want him to leave, but I did have some morals.

"Thanks for understanding, and thanks for the invite. I had a great time, too."

"You're more than welcome," He kissed my forehead before turning to leave.

"Call me when you get home." I said. As I closed the front door, Royce popped up from the sofa. "I thought you were sleeping."

"Yeah, I bet you did. How did it go?"

"Royce, I've got it bad for him."

"Does he know about the baby?"

I kicked off my heels, ignoring his last question.

"Heifer, I know you heard me. Look, Nikole, you're going to have to tell that man what's really going on."

"I know, just not right now."

"When the shit goes down, and believe me, with you," he paused, and pointed in my direction, "shit is always going down, don't say I didn't warn you."

Chapter 21

*A*fter my awesome date with Jackson, I finally admitted to myself that my life was out of control, and that I needed to get myself together. The following afternoon, I decided to sit down with my mom and weigh out all of my options.

I sat across from her and explained how uncomfortable I felt working at Erotic Fantasies, but she just laughed and said something about broke people trying to be picky. But God bless her soul, because she was brainstorming for her baby girl. I tried to get into what she was saying, but after a few minutes I began to zone out.

"Nikole, what's wrong with you?"

"A lot," I sighed.

"Talk to me, girl."

I began to cry as I broke down, and finally shared all of my troubles with my mom, including the abuse from Terrance. I was shocked when she didn't start to bitch, then it hit me.

"You already knew, didn't you?"

"Just waiting for you to come to me and ask for some help. I was trying to let you be a woman and learn how to work through some of your problems without me throwing in my two cents every time." She stood up and grabbed a few paper towels from the counter. "Girl, I knew things weren't right between the two of you. No good comes from messing around with a married man, Nikole," she sighed, before handing me the paper towels.

"Here, wipe your face." she smiled.

"Thanks, Ma."

"Well, from the sound of things, your life is a big ass mess, if you don't mind me saying so. Sometimes it's for the best. I'm not saying that Terrance putting his hands on you was right, but it's time to let go of the past and to move in a different direction."

"I guess."

"Have you figured out how you are going to get back on your feet, since you don't like working for Bebe?"

"Everyone keeps asking me that, but I don't have a clue."

"Well, maybe you need to set aside some time and think about what you would like to see yourself doing while you're hanging out with your son. Remember, Omar? You know, the kid you don't spend a lot of time with, because he's always at my house?"

And the lecture begins, I thought to myself.

"Stop rolling your eyes, Nikole. I'm just telling you the truth. You are always complaining about what Terrance doesn't do, but you're just as bad. Your dad and I are up in age. We've raised you, and now it's time for us to enjoy our lives."

I knew she was right. My mom had been a faithful domestic goddess. She never liked the term housewife. Her career consisted of catering to the needs of my father and me for as long as I can remember. I don't think she ever used her college degree in education.

Daddy upheld his reputation for being the most heartless criminal court judge this side of the Mason-Dixon line for over twenty years before he gave it up for fishing trips to Grand Isle. They had made sure that I had the best things that money could buy: a childhood home in prestigious Concord Estates, name brand clothing, private schooling, Jack and Jill, a new car at sixteen, and I was presented to society as a debutante by the age of seventeen. Yes, growing up as the only child I had the whole shebang, but at what cost?

"Nikole, are you listening to me?" Her fingertip landed on my temple. "Use that beautiful brain that you have."

"Why didn't you ever leave dad?"

"Where did that come from?"

I sighed, "Just answer the question, mom."

"Love can make you do some crazy things, Nikole."

"Like stay with a man that's cheated on you with half of the women in the city? Women who were your sorority sisters, co-workers, church members and friends?"

"What do you want me to say, Nikole?"

"I don't know… I guess I'm just trying to figure out why I'm attracted to married men, and how I ended up with this mess of a life."

"I would hardly call it a mess, and what does your dad have to do with your choices in men?"

"What would you call it, mom? Because it sure isn't a bed of roses. And yes, daddy has everything to do with my choices! It's because of him that I don't trust men, so I try to hurt them before they hurt me. That's why I go for the married ones, because they're someone else's problems, not mine."

"I stayed with your daddy because I love what he represents; money, power, and respect. I love the prestige of being his wife. I like the recognition that people give me because I'm the honorable Judge Freeman's spouse. So, in order to have all of that, I overlook the small stuff like his infidelity." She held her head up high, believing her own lie. "In life you have to pick and chose your battles carefully. I chose to not let his infidelity become a battle."

I reached out and gave her a hug. I felt relieved. I guess admitting my problems and insecurities out loud was the first step towards getting my life back on track. I kissed my mom on the cheek. I still didn't understand why she stayed with my dad, but she had some demons from her past that she needed to deal with, too. Whatever her reasons, she's my mom, and I love her.

"When do you have to be out of your apartment?" My mom perked up.

"By the end of next week."

"Do you have some place to stay?"

"Royce said that Omar and I could crash at his place." My mom wrinkled her nose, and I knew that was out of the question.

"Well, one of our tenants just moved out, so you are welcomed to stay there. It's a condominium in mid-city."

"Mid-city?" It was my turn to wrinkle my nose. I knew that the area was being rejuvenated by a bunch of young buppies, but I wasn't really into the neighborhood revitalization thing, and besides, I knew that my parents had nicer rental properties in some of the better parts of town.

"Do you want to stay in the condo or not?" Her smile began to fade.

"Sure. How much is the rent?"

"First year is free. That should give you a chance to get on your feet and figure out some things about yourself. Are you still driving that rental car?" She peeked out of the kitchen window and frowned.

"Unfortunately."

My mom reached into her pocket and pulled out a key. "Here, you can have the Navigator. Your daddy is supposed to be getting us matching Cadillac's for our thirty-fifth wedding anniversary."

"It's been that long?"

"Blame it on the loving," she teased, but I was serious. She had let this man mess over her for thirty plus years! I was dumbfounded. But when I really thought about it, I really wasn't any different from her when it came to men. Look at how long I had been messing around with Terrance and Brian.

"Mom!"

"Hell, just because I've got some gray hairs in a few unspoken places doesn't mean I'm not getting my groove on, too."

I shivered at the thought of my parents having sex.

"I don't need two vehicles, so you just take the Navigator, and please don't tear the thing up before your father has a chance to change over the paper work."

"Wow, I wasn't expecting all of this when I came over here. I really do appreciate everything."

"So, when were you going to tell me that you are pregnant?"

Just when I thought things were going okay.

"How did you know?"

"Girl, I've been through two pregnancies, my own and yours with Omar. And besides, your nose is getting wider."

"I'm just over two months."

"So, what did Terrance have to say?"

"He's pissed." I wasn't lying because he was upset; I just didn't mention that Terrance wasn't the father.

"I guess so, Nikole, the man is married. I really wish you would just leave him alone and find you someone else. Don't be like the women that your father messes around with. There are a lot of good men out there who are just waiting for a woman like you and who will be faithful."

"Actually, I've started to see someone else."

"Do I know him? This new guy? Who are his people?" She sounded a little too excited.

"His name is Jackson, and he's a DJ for one of the radio stations in town."

"Why can't you date a doctor or a lawyer? Girl, your daddy and I spent all of that money sending you to the most elite schools around here, and you're telling me that you are dating someone who spins records for a living? First a basketball player, and now this."

"He isn't broke, Ma, believe me." I thought back to his magnificent condo and the magical moment that we had shared.

"What's his name, Nikole?"

"Jackson Hebert."

"Is his related to the media Heberts? You know they own several stations in the city." She smiled, as if the thought of her daughter dating their son was just heavenly.

"I don't know, why?"

"Nikole that should have been the first question out of your mouth," She narrowed her eyes at me, "Never mind."

My mom always had a way of making me feel like a little girl verses the grown woman that I am, and this was one of those moments. Now believe me, I was grateful for everything that she had just done for me, but I knew this was also her way of trying to control me. All that talk about finding a good man was just some BS. She was more concerned with who would take me off of her hands versus who would make me happy.

"So, does he know about the baby?" she questioned.

"Yeah, I've told him about Omar."

"Nikole, I'm talking about you being pregnant."

"No, not yet." I held my breath, waiting for her response.

"Good. Who knows, maybe he will believe that the baby is his, and he'll marry you."

I was really ready to go after she made that comment. I had enough problems as it was, and I wasn't about to lie to another man, especially Jackson. I just shrugged my shoulders. "Mom, I am not trying to put a baby on the man."

"And what do you think is going to happen when he finds out that you're pregnant for your suppose-to-be 'ex'?" She shook her head, "I hope you know what you're doing."

Chapter 22

*D*uring the next few days, Jackson and I were inseparable. When we weren't hanging out at each other's place, you could find us chatting on the phone, or text messaging each other, killing time until we were in each other's arms again. So, it was all good when he asked me to drop everything, and join him in Miami for a few days. Of course, my mom complained, but when she realized whom I was going with, she readily agreed to watch Omar 'for the last time'.

"Oh my God, I can't believe that I am on South Beach. Wasn't that Jay Z who just passed by?" I laughed.

"Hey, don't have B come out here and whip up on you over her man."

"Anyway…" I playfully hit his arm.

"Stick with me, the best is yet to come." At that moment I realized just how blessed I was to have this man in my life.

"Thank you so much, Jackson. This is awesome," I gave him a big hug and a passionate kiss on the lips. I wished I could have given him more, but I knew that when the time was right, I would give him my heart and soul.

"I would have majored in radio broadcasting if I would have known about these great job benefits." I joked. We walked hand in hand down the white sandy shore. "You did say that the radio station is paying for this fun filled getaway, right?"

"Well, part of it. I got an upgrade on the hotel accommodations. I figured you were worth it so that's on me."

"What's the real story, Jackson? Tell me how you can do things like this." I swept my hand across the star studded beach as we continued to walk together. This felt so right I smiled to myself. When we returned home I was going to do whatever it took to get my life straight so that he could be in my life forever, starting with ditching both Terrance and Brian for good. I looked over at Jackson who was telling me about his family. *Yeah, we truly belonged together.*

"My stepdad owned FLEX 100, in addition to some other stations throughout the south, before he died a few months ago. He didn't have any kids, and my mom was clueless, so it all fell on me. Before he died, I was his right hand man, his protégé." He looked out into the blue water as a seagull lingered near by.

"My dad was never around, so my stepdad filled in the gap. He was a good guy, did some shit he really didn't have to, like giving me his last name." Jackson looked at me, and then looked out into the water again.

"I usually don't share that information with people. You know how some sisters are, all about the Benjamin's, not the brother that's making them."

"Did you ever think I was one of those females?" This was the moment of truth. Was he really feeling me?

"I wouldn't have told you my story if I did, now would I?" He planted a soft kiss on my lips.

"So, I take it that you don't have any siblings."

"Only child."

"I can relate. I am an only child too, and as for my dad… my mom will never admit it, but he was hardly ever around while I was growing up either. My mom always used his career as an excuse, but I knew better. Everything came to a head my senior year in school, when one of his mistress' kid started attending the same high school as me. It was crazy, we became best friends, and then one day she invited me over to her house. My mom has these personalized plates on her car, and when we got off of the school bus in front of her house, my mom's car was parked out front. Bebe smiled, and started talking about her mom's new boyfriend, this big time judge who was spending mad cash on them." I looked at my feet as I shared one of the many skeletons that filled my family's closet for the first time.

"Damn, Nikole, I didn't know."

"Yeah, it's not like I go around and brag about it. Anyway, to make a long story short, we walked in to find her mom sitting around in some expensive lingerie and my dad all hugged up with her. The next day I got a brand new BMW to keep my mouth shut." I looked out into the water too. "And the funny part of the story is that my mom already knew."

"That was messed up."

"Tell me about it. Bebe was mad at her mom for a long time because she was messing around with a married man, but we never let it affect our friendship." *Or did we?* He smiled while taking my hand into his as we continued to walk along the beach.

"Is that who I think it is?" A man's voice called out to us.

"What's up, man," Jackson reached out and gave the hottest R&B crooner on the planet a pound.

"Chillin'. What are you guys getting into?"

"Anything and everything," Jackson answered coolly.

"I hear you," Jamie smiled in my direction as a form of acknowledgment. "Jackson, get with me before you leave town. I'm working on a project that could use your golden touch."

"I'll do that." Jackson waved as the star walked away.

"Do you know who that was!?" I panted. "That was the guy who played Ray Charles and you just spoke to him like you know him."

"Yeah, Jamie's a cool guy. Now come on, before we're late for the cook out," Jackson pulled me in the direction of our beachfront hotel.

"A cook out? You can't be serious. We're out here hanging with all of these glamorous people, and all you can think about is some barbecue?"

"Fine, I'll go to Latifah's gig alone."

"As in the Queen?"

He laughed, "I bet that will get your butt in gear."

Chapter 23

"Give me one second to change," I mumbled, as I dashed into the bathroom of our luxurious suite to put on a bathing suit that Royce had picked out for me. Glad that my stomach was still slightly flat, despite my recent weight gain. I took a deep breath. *Would he still want me if he knew I was pregnant?* I ran my hand across my stomach. When I got back to Louisiana I needed to get my shit together, quickly. This man deserved better, and I intended to give him what he deserved, a good woman.

"I don't know why you needed to change. You looked fine."

"Please! You must be crazy if you think I'm going to be seen in the same outfit twice," I yelled through the door.

"Just hurry up."

"Okay, I'm ready." I took in some air before reaching for the door handle.

I walked out of the bathroom in a silver, crocheted, two-piece bikini that left little to the imagination.

"My, my, my..." he whispered, as he stepped closer to me.

"I take it that you like it," I modeled the two piece number for him.

"That's an understatement. Come here." He pulled me into his arms. His cologne was intoxicating, and I felt myself getting weak.

"We're going to be late." I whispered.

"When have you ever known Black folks to start something on time?" He lifted me so that our faces were touching. "I want you, Nikole." I swear a million goose bumps had surfaced on my back, because at that moment, I wanted him in the worst way.

Wrapping my arms around his neck, I asked, "How bad?" as my tongue glided inside of his ear.

Gently, he placed me back on my feet and in one sweeping motion my two-piece was lying on the floor in a puddle around my ankles. Surprised by his actions, I forgot that I was holding in my stomach. *Lord, please don't let him notice...*

"You are so beautiful."

"Stop teasing me." I was horny and desperate to feel him inside of me, but the pregnancy made me hesitate. I took a step back.

"Where are you going? Come here," he reached for my hand and pulled me into him. "Let me enjoy this moment." As I stood there, Jackson began to outline my body with his smooth hands.

"You're the kind of woman that could make a man like me settle down." He spoke softly, his words caressing my heart.

"Show me." I looked him squarely in the eyes to see if he was telling me the truth. They were filled with sincerity, and I knew that he was for real.

I touched his hand, and then enclosed mine in his as I led him to the bed. As I sat on the edge, he knelt down in front of me and began to plant cool kisses on my bare vagina.

"Just let me love you, Nikole."

"Okay..." I moaned.

Waiting not a second longer, Jackson began to stroke my sweetness with his tongue.

"Don't stop, baby," I cried out. "Please don't stop…" I placed both of my hands on his head as my legs rested on his shoulders. My body began to convulse as I tried to control the orgasms that were taking over.

Without breaking the momentum, Jackson's hands cupped my ass as he tried to pull me in further. Coming up for air, he began to rub the tips of my nipples in a circular motion.

"Please, Jackson." My eyes had rolled back in my head before I could even finish the sentence. I felt like a fiend taking a hit.

My hands moved to my mound of pleasure as I began to fondle myself. No man had ever made me feel this way before. I was about to explode.

"Nikole…"

"Yes? Yes!"

I tried to reach for his swimming trunks, but he moved my hand away.

"What are you trying to do?" I asked.

"What do you think?" He sucked on one of my breasts like an infant trying to breast feed.

The fire that had developed between my legs was overwhelming, and I couldn't contain myself any longer. He must have read my mind because the second time I reached for his shorts, he didn't push me away. I lay down across the bed as my body began to ache with pleasure at the mere thought of feeling his skin next to mine.

"Put it in. Please, Jackson, just put it in."

As if we were made for each other, he climbed on top and then glided flawlessly inside of me.

"Tell me how you like it, Nikole. Tell me what makes you feel good."

My response was a sensual moan.

"Talk to me, Nikole," he whispered in my ear while stroking my hair, his body filling me up with pleasure. I was so weak with desire that I couldn't respond. Instead, I arched my back, welcoming him to go deeper.

Changing positions, my rear end was suddenly in the air as Jackson tried to break my back. Good sex can make you lose your mind, and believe me; I was pleading temporary insanity at this very moment.

His hands gripped the headboard as he continued to thrust himself in and out of me. I clutched the sheets, hanging on for the ride of my life.

"Why are you doing this to me?" Jackson bellowed.

"What...?" I panted.

"Making me fall in love," he whispered, as we climaxed together.

Chapter 24

*T*he trip to Miami was mind-blowing, and I couldn't wait until I got home to call Royce and finish telling him all about it. The man had called me everyday that I was there, trying to get as much information out of me as he possibly could. As Jackson approached my complex, I noticed that Terrance's Cutlass was parked out front. I was not in the mood to deal with him today, come to think of it, never again. The only man that I wanted in my life was Jackson. I looked over at him in the driver's seat and smiled.

"Hey, drop me off here." I pointed towards the complex mailboxes, which were only a few feet away from my apartment building. *This is the last time that I am going to lie to this man. I swear...* "I need to check my mailbox before heading inside, and I don't want to keep you waiting."

"It's not a problem, Nikole. I'm not in a rush to get back to the station."

"No, you can go, and I'll just give you a call after I've settled in and picked up my son."

"Come here..." He reached across the SUV to take me into his arms. "I meant what I said in Miami. You're the kind of woman that can make a man fall in love and settle down."

Our lips locked in a passionate kiss before I broke the embrace and grabbed my Louis Vuitton overnight bag from the back seat.

"I'll call you later! I promise." I kissed him again and exited the vehicle.

After the coast was clear, I hesitantly walked towards my apartment, but was abruptly interrupted by Mrs. Domaine wanting to talk about her dog drama. Any other time I would have been annoyed, but today I was actually relieved to see those pink foam rollers bouncing around on top of her head. We chatted for a few moments before she rushed off to her soap operas. Nervously I opened the door to find an impatient Terrance sitting on my sofa. Glad that his back was facing the door; I gently placed the overnight bag behind it and walked around to face him.

"How did you get in?"

"I guess you forgot who co-signed for this place." *Oh, so now you want to accept some responsibilities around here. Cocky ass.*

"And they let you in?"

"Didn't I just say that my name is on the lease, Nikole?"

"Chill out, I just asked you a question." I sucked my teeth. "And did they tell you that we were being evicted because we haven't paid our rent for the last two months?"

"Sit down," he demanded.

"Why are you here, Terrance?"

"Where have you been, Nikole?"

"Don't answer a question with a question."

"This ain't no fucking game, Nikole. Now, I'm going to ask your ass again…" His entire six foot, five inch frame began to rise up from the sofa. "Where in the fuck have you been?" His voice was filled with venom. I had obviously seen this side of him before, but instead of being scared I said what was on my mind.

"Terrance, we're finished. I'm tired of the games. I'm tired of waiting for you to divorce your wife, and I'm tired of you putting your hands on me. Now, if you don't mind, please leave."

"What? See, you let that nigga fuck with your head."

"Just leave, Terrance. No drama, no more empty promises, just get the hell out of my life, okay?"

"After all of the shit that I've done for you, you think you're just going to walk in here after fucking some other dude all weekend, and feed me some bullshit about it's over?" He began to unbuckle his belt.

"What do you think you're doing?" My eyes grew to the size of saucers, and against my will, my body tensed up with raw fear. *He wouldn't!*

"Teaching your ungrateful ass a lesson," The first lick landed on my legs as I felt him pulling my arm and twisting my body around. "What you fail to realize is that I'm the only one who loves you."

I felt a sharp sting slice at the tender meat of my butt. *Why did I wear these damn shorts?* "Terrance, you're hurting me," I cried out, in a panic. I tried to wrench my arm away from him, desperately fighting to free myself. My mind was filled with a million thoughts at once, but the one that stood out the most was that Royce wasn't joking. *This man is going to kill me.*

"I've been calling you all weekend!" *Swish.* "Was his dick that good that you couldn't take a break to answer my damn calls?" *Swish, Swish.*

Fiery, stinging pain attacked my senses. A world of agony engulfed me and demolished the high spirits that had been prevalent just moments before. I knew I should have just answered when he called, but instead, I sent all of his calls straight to voice mail before finally turning the damn thing off. The only person I was concerned about while I was away was my son, and I called my mom from a landline phone to check on him. I wanted to enjoy all of the attention that I was receiving from a wonderful man and not have to deal with a beast, like Terrance.

"*Terrance, please stop!*" I cried out in pain. I felt faint with the agony of his repetitive torture.

"You ain't shit, Nikole." *Swish, Swish, Swish.*

"*Why are you hurting me?*" My body was racked with uncontrollable sobs. "*Why are you always hurting me?!*" I could feel the welts beginning to form on my legs and backside. Here I was, a grown woman, taking a beating from this maniac. *Lord, if you get me out of this mess, I promise I will stop messing around with married men!* The deadliness of Terrance's voice interrupted my fervent praying.

"Because you need to be reminded that I'm the fucking man around here! Do you understand me, Nikole?!" His face shook with the effort of taking his rage out on my vulnerable flesh. Sweat dropped off his forehead onto my burning skin.

I thought I heard someone knocking on the door, then the rattle of the doorknob. Faintly, I remember hearing Mrs. Domaine's voice. For once, she sounded like an angel. *Swish, Swish, Swish, Swish.* The sound of the belt whirled through my head as he continued to beat me. All I could do, as I shut my eyes against the torment, was hope that God heard me before it was too late.

Chapter 25

*I*t felt like forever before Terrance finally stopped whipping me and left, satisfied that I had been brought to my knees in respect of him. After the beating, Mrs. Domaine found me curled in the fetal position on my living room floor with welts covering my back and legs. After her gruesome discovery, she tried to tell me that she was going to call the police, but I begged her to just call Royce, who immediately raced over to see about me.

"That's it, Nikole, I don't care what you say. We're calling the police."

"*NO!*" I shivered, as he dropped the phone and pulled me into a warm embrace. The tears and snot ran from my face onto his designer shirt. To his credit, he didn't seem to care.

"What are you scared of, Nikole?" Mrs. Domaine asked as she returned to my apartment with a first aid kit in her possession, ready to nurse me back to life.

"I'm not scared." I sniffed, trying to compose myself for my friend and my neighbor. "I'm just going to deal with him on my own terms."

"And what terms are those, Nikole?!" Royce held me away from him and looked into my eyes.

"Doesn't matter. Do you have my back?" I heard my voice growing stronger.

"I know you see me as just some nosey old woman who doesn't have any business of her own, but there have been many days and nights when I've heard the two of you from across the breezeway. Baby, it never sounded like it did today. I thought he was going to kill you."

"Thank you for looking out for me, Mrs. Domaine. I think you may have actually saved my life," I wiped my eyes with the back of my hands and rose from the sofa.

Vengeance burned in my eyes. The bitch in me was about to come out and Terrance was the no-good-ass man to blame. Tired of getting played, the time had come to turn the tables and let the real muthafucking games begin!

"Royce...do you have my back?"

I didn't wait for a response as I headed upstairs to change, because I already knew what the answer was.

Later that night, after flirting with the gate attendant, Royce and I pulled into the apartment complex that Terrance shared with Mercedes. Since my mom was tripping about watching Omar, I had to solicit the help of the temporary secretary's teenage daughter, who was trying to earn a few extra bucks for her senior trip.

I parked next to the infamous Range Rover, then reached into the back seat of the rental and retrieved an Albertson shopping bag.

"Nikole, I think this is a bad idea."

"Damn, Royce, I don't want to hear that shit right now." I snapped angrily, my emotions clouding my better judgment. I glanced around suspiciously.

"Look, you know for a fact that Mercedes and Terrance are both crazy."

"Mercedes is just fronting. Now let's do this..."

"I sure hope you know what you're doing." Royce sighed, hesitantly.

"Do you want me to show you the bruises on my ass again, and then you can tell me if you think I'm serious or not?!"

"Girl, with some make up…"

"Royce!"

"Okay, which one do you want first? The sugar or the eggs?" He held up his hands, displaying each of the items that he had retrieved from the white plastic bag as we exited the car.

"Hell, both."

"It's your party, girlfriend."

And party I did. Royce watched as I put on a pair of gloves and carefully removed the gas cap off of Terrance's Cutlass.

"Are you taking notes?" I grinned, maniacally.

"You are going to get us both locked up for this madness, if trespassing and disturbing the peace doesn't first." Royce impatiently crossed his arms, as he looked around, bound with nervous tension. I dumped half a dozen eggs and a pound of sugar into Terrance's gas tank. As a pair of headlights began to approach, I quickly replaced the cap and pulled Royce down to the ground so that we wouldn't be spotted.

"And where did you pick up this little trade?" He spoke through clenched teeth.

"The class is called Pay Back 101." I smirked.

Looking around, Royce snatched me up from my comfortable squatting position next to the Cutlass. "Okay, the coast is clear. Come on girlfriend, let's get out of here."

"Hold on, brother. Who said I was finished?"

"Excuse me! What are you about to do now?"

"Here, hold this." I reached into a black backpack that was on the backseat of the rental and pulled out a can of spray paint.

"Nikole…"

"Yes?" I sang back.

"Do I even want to know what you are about to do?"

"Damn, Royce, do I have to spell everything out for you? We're going to spray paint Mercedes' SUV," I gave the driver's side door of the Range Rover a loving pat.

"*We* ain't doing a damn thing, *you* are. Evidently *you* haven't been to jail lately." Royce cut his eyes at me. "And how do you know that's her car?"

"Because it's parked outside of their complex, next to the Cutlass, and I saw her husband driving it the other day."

"I'm not in this, but you can go right ahead," He encouraged me with a slight nudge of his head. "And what is it that you are going to spray on her car, smart ass?"

"Oh, I don't know… Psycho? Number one bitch? Crazy? Pussy Licker? Hell, I'll think of something!"

"Those sound like compliments to me," Royce shook his head in disbelief, but before he knew it, I was shaking the can while considering my options for the perfect tag.

"We are going to go to jail…" Royce looked around nervously again.

Pushing up the sleeves of my Baby Phat jacket, I began to create a masterpiece on the side of the Range Rover.

"I must say," Royce patted me on the back after I had finished, "I didn't think you had it in you girl. Now, can we please get the hell out of here?"

Chapter 26

*T*hat Thursday we were on the grind, trying to wrap up some last minute details. I hadn't returned the rental car, because I still didn't have the money to pay Budget. After the party on Friday night, though, I was going to be straight. Hell, I'd have to be, because Friday was going to be my last night working for Erotic Fantasies. Jackson and Royce were pushing me to start a t-shirt business. Together we had put together a business plan that would be my guide for the next two to three years. I was excited about the future, and couldn't wait to be away from Bebe and all of this drama. I still hadn't told Jackson about the pregnancy, but I was also planning to tackle that issue this weekend. Something in my spirit kept telling me that he would understand. Maybe together we could make the right decision about my predicament.

I was trying to wrap up a few things before Jackson and I went out to dinner, and then head over to Bebe's house for a final walk through with the set designer that she had hired. Brian and Terrance had called so much that the battery on my cell phone was almost dead, so I instructed Karizma, the temp, to just forward all of my calls to my voice mail, just in case they tried to call me at work. I didn't feel like hearing Brian tell me what I needed to do, nor did I want to hear

Terrance bitch about how he knew I had messed up his wife's SUV.

Jackson was waiting in the break room as I hurriedly tried to pack some of the products into a box to take over to Bebe's. I was on my knees, fighting with the overstuffed box, when this baritone voice startled me from behind.

"Where's Bebe?"

I turned my head to find, standing before me, a man that was half of my five foot, two inch frame. He was dressed from head to toe in a purple alligator suit, and from the looks of things, he appeared to be having a temper tantrum. He was stomping his alligator covered foot, demanding some attention. *If he knew how he looked, he'd go and sit down somewhere,* I thought to myself, chuckling at the sight of him.

"I know you MF's hear me up in here! Y'all just want a brotha to act a fool." He whipped his permed, shoulder length hair to the side, before he came closer to me. "I said where is Bebe?" His sleek, manicured nail was right between my eyes.

"Look, shorty, I don't know what your problem is." I glared back at him.

Retrieving his finger, he adjusted his volume, "I need to speak with Bebe." He flipped his hair across his shoulder again, and then adjusted his blazer.

My smile faded. I really wasn't in the mood for his dramatics. Just as I was getting ready to stand up and give him a good piece of my mind, Royce walked in.

"Is there a problem, Slim?"

"Bebe trying to play me, that's what, and I don't appreciate that shit! My hoes are worth more money than she's trying to pay me."

"She signed a contract with *them*, not *you*, sweetheart. She's not planning to give you a dime." Royce answered calmly.

"They work for me! They can't do shit unless I say so."

"Slim, it's called freelance work." Royce sighed, apparently bored with this entire conversation and the sight of this man.

Slim looked confused, so Royce restated what was going on with the girls.

"They are moonlighting on your ass. Working a second job. Call it whatever you want to, Slim."

"See, that's what I'm talking about. They can't be doing shit like that. They work for me, and I'm the only mutherfucka that can dish out the dough. You tell Bebe I don't appreciate her going over my head."

"Well, that's not very hard." Bebe appeared out of nowhere. Suddenly, she towered over the small man with her hand on her hip.

"Give me some space." Slim took two steps back. "That was fucked up, Bebe."

"I know you ain't up in my office trying to act a fool over no strippers trying to get their hustle on." *Whoa! Look at Bebe trying to get out the box. I didn't realize that you still had some of the ghetto running through your blood.* Then I thought about the magazine and all of the drama that Mercedes was putting me through. I narrowed my eyes at Bebe. *Yeah, little man isn't the only one who has some issues with you.*

"How you just gonna cut me out? What about my fee? I ain't getting nothing out of this, Bebe. You hear me, absolutely nothing!" He stomped his foot again. "And those are my hoes you gonna have up there shaking their titties. They work for me!"

"Well, tomorrow night, they are working for Erotic Fantasies. Now if you have a problem, take it up with their union, Hoes R' Us." Bebe retorted.

The alligator foot stomped again, before he huffed out of the office. "Y'all don't know who y'all fucking with. We gonna see about this."

"Somebody needs to report him to PETA." Royce smirked. "That's a damn shame how they killed that baby alligator just to make a suit that would fit him." We all laughed at his expense.

"You need to quit," I joined in, "but he does look like that guy off of Next Friday."

"Money Mike!" Bebe laughed. "Girl, Slim swears he's a pimp. Ain't gonna do a damn thing, but run his mouth. What woman is going to be scared of him?" She lowered her hand to her knee, signifying his height. *"Puh-leeze!"*

It was getting harder and harder to fake being nice to her, but I had to admit that it was nice to enjoy a stress free laugh with everyone. Too bad it had to be short lived.

Chapter 27

*Y*ou know how you can feel the presence of evil? Well, I felt Terrance before he even opened his mouth.

"Nikole, why is there a big ass U-Haul truck parked in front of your apartment, and where are you going with my son?" The last person I wanted to deal with right now was walking through the lobby entrance of Erotic Fantasies. *Where in the hell was Karizma, and how in the world did he get through the door?*

"What do you want, Terrance?"

"You planning on moving in with *him*?" I followed his eyes to the break room entrance.

"Shit." I mumbled. Jackson was heading in our direction.

"Answer me, Nikole." He charged in my direction with both of his hands balled into fists.

"You've got a lot of nerve coming to my job accusing me of some foolishness!"

"Well, is it true?"

"Maybe I should be asking you how in the hell you can afford a Range Rover, but can't seem to pay your child support on time! And don't get me started on your psycho wife that insists on stalking me!" I planted my hands on my hips.

"What's up, man?" Jackson checked Terrance as he took his post next to me. "Is there a problem?"

"You tell me." Terrance sneered.

"Say man, lower your voice. This is a place of business."

"Man, fuck you! Nikole, I don't want him around my son."

"Negro, please! This isn't about Omar. This is about you finally losing control over me."

"You're a trip."

"What!?"

"Yeah, he's probably the real father of your baby, and you're just trying to put that shit off on me."

My eyes widened in disbelief. "Terrance, you don't know what in the hell you're talking about."

"Excuse me?" Jackson replied, as I stood there turning five shades of red. *Terrance was wrong for that shit and he knew it.*

"Oh, you ain't got shit to say now." His fingers flexed. "Yeah, don't think I didn't see you all up on him at that reggae concert. Oh, what's up, Bebe?" I glanced over my shoulder only to find all of the employees of Erotic Fantasies in my business.

"Nikole, what is he talking about?" Now Jackson was looking at me all crazy.

"You know what I'm talking about. Shit, ain't no telling how long ya'll been sleeping around. Hell, Nikole has screwed so many people she probably doesn't even know who the damn father is herself."

"Nikole, is there something you should be telling me?" Jackson interjected.

"Why you had to go there, Terrance?" I took a step forward with my finger pointed in the direction of his face. Tears were welding up in my eyes I was so damn mad at him.

"Don't do something you might regret."

The sound of glass being broken on the outside interrupted our argument.

"For Slim's sake, all of my car windows had better be in one piece." Bebe growled as we all forgot about my pressing situation and ran out of the building to investigate.   To our surprise, Slim was nowhere in sight. Instead, we were staring at a deranged looking Mercedes, who was dressed for the occasion of bashing out the windows to the rental car that I was driving. Dressed down in an all black running outfit that was hugging every curve of her body, she sported matching Nikes to complete the ensemble. The fair skinned woman paused for only a split second before she swung the bat again, and it came crashing down on the poor Hyundai. As I surveyed the damage, it appeared that she had taken care of the tires first. All four had already been slashed.

"What in the hell are you doing?" I screamed, knowing that Budget Rental would definitely be looking to put me on lock down now.

"Uh, Nikole, I wouldn't bother her right now. The woman is carrying a baseball bat." Royce lightly touched my arm.

"That's not even my car!" I shook my head from side to side in disbelief.

"Speaking of cars, why are you still driving that damn rental car anyway?"

"Royce, this is not the time."

"Go call the police, Royce." Bebe took charge, as usual.

"Mercedes put the damn bat down!" Terrance yelled.

Her adrenaline was so high that she just could not stop. After Mercedes finished with the four windows, I watched in horror as she proceeded to bang on the body of the car.

"This bitch is crazy!" I charged after her, but I felt Jackson pulling me back.

"She ain't worth that trip to parish prison today."

"Really, and you have a kid to think about." Royce had returned to our sides.

"But look at the car! I don't have the money to pay for this!"

"We'll worry about all of that later." Bebe continued.

"You thought I was just gonna sit back and let you disrespect me, fuck my husband, and then dare to come to my house and fuck up my shit!" She spat out the words as her eyes cut through me like a knife. This wasn't supposed to turn out like this.

"Oh shit." Royce whispered. It had dawned on him that she knew who messed up her SUV.

"And I told you to leave his ass alone!" She kicked the driver side door, leaving a dent and her shoeprint as another reminder of her fury.

"Damn, Nikole, how does she know?" You could tell that Royce was really concerned about spending a night in jail.

As if on cue, psycho dropped her weapon and just glared at the five of us. She reminded me of the bride of Frankenstein with her coiffure hairdo that had gone astray. She had taken a fighters stance and was ready to do battle with any of us.

"This is between Nikole and me," She challenged everyone else.

"Mercedes, go home." Bebe interjected.

"Like I said, this shit is between the two of us." She pointed a broken acrylic nail at me.

"Like I told your dumb ass before, I ain't the person you got a problem with. You need to be bringing all of this drama to Terrance and leave me the hell alone." I screamed, trying to break free from the hold Jackson still had on me.

"Calm down, Nikole, and just go back inside." He held me tighter.

"Don't hold her ass back." Mercedes took a few steps forward. Her fists were still tight, ready to jab away.

"Ain't nobody scared of your crazy ass, Mercedes. I thought you would have gotten the picture by now." My anger was mounting, and I could feel my blood pressure rise. Terrance may have just ended my relationship with Jackson by revealing my pregnancy, and now Mercedes was about to get me thrown into jail over this stupid piece of car. I was ready to let loose some serious pent up energy on her face.

"You're talking a whole lot of shit." she glared.

"Listen, honey," Royce interrupted. "I called the police."

"And? What? Am I supposed to be scared?"

"Don't make me cut your ass out here." Royce challenged Mercedes.

"You need to go and sit your punk ass down."

"That's it…" Royce made a move for his pocket, but Jackson reached for his arm. When he did, I broke away and charged after Mercedes.

"You crazy bitch…" I backslapped her square in the face.

"I got your *crazy*, and your *bitch*." She swung at me, and her fist connected with my jaw. "I thought you knew!" Her fist hit my face again with unbelievable force.

I managed to grab her hair, and I swung her to the ground before lunging towards her.

"I hate you." I punched her in the face. "You're the reason my life is so fucked up, because you took my man. I was supposed to marry Terrance, not your dumb ass."

Mercedes rolled from under me, and some how she ended up back on top. She let loose and wailed on me, punches landing on my face left and right. "You trick ass ho. Maybe he didn't want your stank ass."

I somehow managed to dislodge Mercedes from me, and scrambled to my feet. I got in a few more licks and scratches, before I finally grabbed the side of her face and just bit the hell out of her. That didn't stop her. She continued to swing like a mad woman. Before we knew it, the fight was over, and of all people, Terrance was pulling us apart.

"Let me go, Terrance," Mercedes yelled.

"You need to keep your wife on a fucking leash." I stated, then reared back and spit in her face, coating her cheek and eye with my hot saliva.

"This ain't over with, Nikole. Believe that!" Mercedes struggled to free herself from his grasp, while disgustedly wiping my loogie from her face.

"You're the stupid one. Hell, look who he's married to! It sure isn't you or Miss Wanna-be Kimora Lee Simmons." Her eyes were like daggers aimed straight for my head. "You've just made me your worst nightmare!" She pointed a threatening finger in my direction while her other hand cradled her face.

Terrance just stood there holding Mercedes back, but the look on his face told me that if we were in a different place, it would have been him trying to kick my ass all over the place, instead of his wife.

"I told you to leave that damn man alone," Bebe shook her head. "But you just wouldn't listen." I wanted to scream, *this is all your fault, bitch so shut the fuck up!* But I remembered that Jackson was still standing there, and I already had a bunch of explaining to do, so I just held my tongue in my cheek.

"Nikole, you're right. She is crazy. And where are the police?!" Royce whispered into the muggy afternoon air. And as if on cue, an officer pulled into the parking lot.

"Thank goodness." Royce walked over to greet the gentleman.

"And as for you being pregnant!" Mercedes continued to try and ruin my life even more than she already had, "Terrance had his shit fixed, so you need to finish going down your trick list until you find the real daddy, bitch!" As I stood there in shock, the police officer approached us. *Damn, damn, damn! So, that was how he knew I was screwing around on him. He'd known this wasn't his baby all along!*

"You really did a number on this one, Mercedes." The officer let out a slow whistle. "Alright, you know the routine. Hands behind your back."

"What about her?" She cut her eyes in my direction. "You ain't gonna arrest her?"

"Excuse me? Did I miss something? Did she do something to you out here?" he asked.

"She fucking bit me."

"Sounds like a personal problem. Now get in the car, Mercedes." He gave her a little shove as she climbed into the back seat of his patrol car. The officer excused himself for a few minutes while he tended to some paper work, talked to Terrance, and read Mercedes her rights.

"Budget is going to kill me." I moaned.

"If Mercedes doesn't get to you first," Bebe shot back. "Look, I'm not trying to get in your affairs, but when your personal life starts coming to my place of business, it doesn't look good. You need to make some decisions about Terrance. Is this how you want to spend the rest of your life, playing second to a deranged wife, being known as the mistress? I think you deserve better."

I was one second away from slapping the hell out of her righteous ass, but Jackson saved her.

"Nikole... we need to talk."

I peered around Bebe to find Jackson looking heated. "Look, can we talk about this later? I can explain everything, but not here, okay?"

"You *are* joking, right?"

More silence. *Hell, what could I say?*

"I can't believe you put me in the middle of this bullshit." Jackson measured each word.

"What!? Hold up. I didn't put you in the middle of anything. You knew about Terrance. And why are you getting mad at me?"

"Because you didn't see anything wrong with messing around with that woman's husband," He pointed in the direction of Terrance and Mercedes. "Because you are still fucking your baby's daddy. And because I just spent the weekend in Miami with a woman I thought was beyond games, only to find out that she's pregnant for another man. Not to mention, the nigga she thought she was pregnant for had his shit nipped!" Small droplets of spittle flew from Jackson's lips as he schooled me. I had never seen him so angry.

"You don't understand."

"Understand what, Nikole? That if they wouldn't have showed up today, you wouldn't have told me this much?"

I dropped my head in shame.

"Come on, Nikole. Do I look that stupid to you?" He started walking towards his car.

"Wait, don't leave!" I cried.

"And why the hell not?! I thought you were my woman," he pounded his chest. "I thought you were special, to only find out that you've been fucking not only me, but every body else! Now you want me to understand?"

"Jackson, please wait!" I jumped in his path.

"You know what's crazy…? Sistas are always complaining about how there are no good Black men out here, but when you finally find one you don't know how to act. Ya'll fuck over us; pull us into drama like this." Jackson flexed his hands, then shook his head. "Look, you had your chance… I'm out of here," he stated, with harsh finality. He brushed past me as I stood there with tears in my eyes.

"Ladies, I'm sorry to break up your little party, but this here vehicle was reported stolen by Budget Rental Car. I'm going to have to take a Miss Nikole Freeman in, too."

"What?!" I screamed. "This is some kinda joke, right?"

"Afraid not." The officer smiled, enjoying the moment. "So, I take it from your reaction that you're Miss Freeman. If you don't mind, hands behind your back."

"I know, go call your daddy," Royce huffed, as he turned to go back into the office.

"Don't worry, I'll call Brian. He's an asshole, but he can use his connections at the district attorney's office, and possibly have you out in a few hours." Bebe tried to comfort me. *Brian?! A few hours? What in the hell was she talking about?! And what did she mean by a few hours?*

Chapter 28

Sitting in a stank jail cell for six hours was a big reality check for me, and since judges don't hear cases at night, I had to wait until the following morning before my dad could pull a few strings. He posted my bail, and then gave me a long lecture about how he was tired of wasting his money on my shortcomings. As expected, Brian was a no show, but since he hadn't come through on the other deal, I really didn't expect for him to show up and bail me out of this trouble.

During my holding period, I had a lot of time to think about my life, and how I could rectify some of my wrongs. First thing Monday morning, I was going to cash my paycheck, then drag Royce with me to the nearest abortion clinic. Deep down, I didn't really want to have one, but it didn't make any sense for me to bring another kid into this world from a relationship that was built on lies and deceit. I also thought about what my mom had said, and I promised myself that once I got out of that dungeon I would spend more time with my precious son. Life was too short. My final goal was to find a damn good therapist, because after all of this drama was over with, I was going to need one.

Lucky for me, Royce had lived up to his promise, and when I arrived back at my apartment, all of my belongings had been packed and moved to my new place. This allowed me enough time to clean up, say goodbye to Mrs. Domaine, and go home and shower before taking my butt over to Bebe's house for the fun party. *Hell, drama or no drama, I still needed my damn paycheck.*

I tried to call Jackson on his cell phone, but he never answered. Instead of leaving a voice message, I simply hung up. As I dug through my packed clothing trying to recover a decent pair of jeans that I could rock tonight, my cell phone began to ring. Hoping it was Jackson, I answered without checking the caller ID.

"Look, I'm sorry about last night." I began, hoping he wouldn't hang up on me before I could fully explain.

"Nikole?" The caller asked.

"Yeah," I struggled to place the woman's voice. "Dr. Williams?"

"Yes, Nikole, this is Dr. Williams."

"Oh, hi," My heart sank in disappointment.

"Did I catch you at a bad time?"

"No, not really. What's wrong?" I nervously asked.

"I apologize for not calling you with this information sooner, but I've been out of town. Anyway, I got the results in from those tests that we ran…"

"Okay?"

"Can you come in on Monday?"

"Sure, but can't you just tell me over the telephone?"

"Well… I'd like to do another ultrasound to confirm a few things."

"What's wrong, Dr. Williams?" I could feel my heart about to jump out of my chest. I know it sounds crazy, there I was planning to have an abortion, but I was still concerned about the baby.

She took a deep breath, "Nikole, I am afraid that you're not pregnant."

"What! But that's impossible." I lost my balance and collapsed on my unmade bed. "I took a home pregnancy test, and then another one at your office and they all came back positive! What about my missed period and the morning sickness?" I rambled. "And I've begun to gain weight."

"What you have is an anembryonic gestation."

"I don't understand. What happened...?"

"You conceived, but there is no growing fetus."

"Ohmygoodness..." I mumbled.

"Are you okay Nikole?"

"Is this because of an STD?" I thought about Brian giving Bebe crabs.

"No, remember, I tested you for STD's, and your results came back negative." She spoke to me slowly and carefully, as if she were talking to a child.

"Can I have kids in the future?"

"Most certainly. This isn't genetic, so you shouldn't have any problems with future conceptions."

I tried to keep my emotions at bay by telling myself, *I guess what goes around comes around.* Maybe this was God's way of reminding me about karma or a blessing in disguise. That didn't seem to help staunch the flow of tears that betrayed me, dropping onto the very bed that had been my accomplice as I had done my dirt.

Chapter 29

"Shake your money maker like somebody's bout to pay ya..." Bebe was so impressed with Boy Wonder at Jackson's birthday party that she had hired him to DJ for the Fun Party tonight, and let me tell you, he was off the hook. The crowd was going wild, and the strippers were working their bodies all over the rooms. I had to give it to her, this had turned out better than I could have ever imagined. Once you walked through the door, you were no longer in Louisiana, but on an exotic island living out your wildest fantasies.

"Welcome to Erotic Fantasies," Royce purred as each guest entered the door. Dressed in a white custom tailored silk suit with a dashing black tie to match, the man had women flocking all over him. Hmm, if they only knew that he wasn't a fish and chips kind of guy. His sidekick for the night wasn't bad, either. With his hair slicked back in a ponytail, Slim was rocking the house in a white snakeskin suit with the shoes to match, of course. He had come to an agreement with Bebe. She was allowing him to make his cut by playing the role of Tattoo. *Now what kind of shit was that?*

"What's up, guys?" I smiled at Royce and Slim.

"Your fine ass." Slim looked at me suggestively.

"As if you haven't been busy enough," I teased back.

"Slim, baby, can you come over here and show me how this vibrator works?" A sexy vixen cooed in the background. Royce and I laughed uncontrollably as Slim strutted over to the young lady.

"Are her parties always this wild?" I looked around still trying to take in the naughty scenes that were unfolding right before my eyes.

"I tried to tell you," Royce laughed.

Bebe's crib was packed with some of everybody, from young couples to old ladies on a vacation from the local nursing homes. For at least one night, Bebe had managed to erase racism, because her guests varied in shades ranging from vanilla to dark mocha.

"Did you see Night Queen working that pole a few minutes ago? I swear I saw a few people having orgasms in their seats." Royce pointed in the direction of the stage that now took up half of Bebe's family room. "Honey, like I told you before, anything goes at one of these parties, because Bebe caters to people's fantasies." Royce glided his hand through the air to emphasize his point.

"Well, I hope she caters to mine and coughs up my pay check tonight."

"Don't worry. Say, have you checked out the theme rooms upstairs?"

"No, but I did see the hall of mirrors when I came in through the back entrance," I shook my head. "It looks like she has video cameras set up too?"

"Yes, indeed. Now you know these freaks are willing to pay for their own private flicks."

"Damn opportunist."

"So, what's your role for tonight?" Royce eyed me from head to toe.

"Walking around, barking orders to everyone through this headset, and making sure this party continues to run smoothly."

"I like the tank tops that you designed for the girls. I hope you billed Erotic Fantasies for those babies."

I looked down and remembered the shirts that I had designed. Smiling, I replied, "And you know I did, homeboy."

"So, you can use your brain after all," he teased. "I hope you're still serious about doing your own thing. Hell, if Bebe can pull something like this off, just imagine what you can do."

"I hope you're right."

"I wouldn't have suggested you making that kind of move if I didn't think it was possible."

"I guess."

"Damn, Nikole, if you don't start believing in yourself, than who will?" He was right, but I guess in my heart I thought Jackson would be the one to cheer me on. It had only been one day, but I missed him already. Just thinking about him not being around anymore was starting to bring me down.

"You make a good point, Royce," I reached out and gave him a big hug. In the end, I guess Royce was always the only one who really cared about my well being.

"I always do." He smiled. "Now let's get back to work."

"Get it girl, get, get, get, get it girl..." Sounds of the 2 Live Crew began to fill the air as I swung by the DJ booth to make sure Boy Wonder was okay.

"Do you need anything?" I screamed above the music.

Eyeing me like a piece of candy, he answered with a slight attitude, "Naw, I'm straight for now, but holler at a brother later on." He turned his attention back to his turntables and began spinning *I Need a Freak* by 2 Short. I wondered what had gotten into him. I was used to him sweatin' me. His change in attitude was very suspect, as if he knew something that I didn't.

As I was leaving the DJ booth, Bebe approached me. Tonight she was sporting a black linen suit, with some slammin' Jimmy Choo heels. Her hair was pulled back in a simple bun, and her makeup was flawless. Now, *this* was how Bebe was supposed to dress.

"So, what do you think about the party so far?"

"Not what I was expecting." I looked around the expansive family room that had been converted into a strip club for the night, "Big turn out."

"Biggest ever. I've already cleared six grand and the night is still young."

"Come on, let's go and check out the upstairs sales rooms and see how much these undercover freaks are spending."

"Look who's trying to call somebody a freak." I half teased.

"Shit, I never said I wasn't a freak, but I sure ain't undercover." She laughed as we headed upstairs to check out the rooms where the products were being sold.

"Promiscuous girl, you're teasing me. You've got what I want, and you know what I need..."

"Girl, you must have paid Wonder a grip because he is jamming."

"Shit, for that price he better not think about taking a break up in here." She looked in his direction with a serious expression on her face.

Rounding the winding staircase, we were able to take in all of the action. As I surveyed my surroundings, I spotted a woman flashing another guest on the main floor.

"What is she doing?" I pointed in the direction of the bold partygoer who was now below us.

"I hope her ass is demonstrating how good that 'bump away' product works. She buys the stuff like it's going out of style."

"What in the hell is bump away?"

"I see somebody didn't do their homework. It keeps you from getting hair bumps after having a Brazilian wax."

"So, you mean to tell me that she's showing off her cat?" I gasped, naively.

"Best way to let someone know how well a product works is if you show them the results, don't you think?"

"That's some nasty stuff, if you ask me."

"What did you expect? After all, this is Fantasy Island."

"It sure in the hell wasn't this." I replied as we cut in front of the line that had formed outside of the joy ride room.

"Ladies, how is everything going?" Bebe asked in an upbeat voice. A lesbian couple was wrapping up their purchase when we approached the table.

"Great," Royce replied while handing them their tiger print bag. "They are buying this stuff like it's going out of style. Adding the private purchasing rooms was a great idea, Bebe."

"Hey, I thought you were working the front door?" I asked.

"That got boring, so I let Mrs. Domaine take over when she got here."

"My neighbor!? Royce stop lying."

"Girl, while you were upstairs changing into your fuck-up-a-car outfit, Mrs. D was telling me that her pension check wasn't covering her monthly expenses anymore and that she needed a second job."

"And she's one of our best forms of advertisement, too." Bebe chimed in. "She brought some of her friends with her tonight." She smiled. I rolled my eyes, but caught myself when Royce's head started to twitch, signaling me to 'cool it'.

"So, Royce, what are those numbers?" Bebe returned to business. She looked at him expectantly.

"Honey, you are going to die. How does eight thousand sound?"

"Like money in the bank, and a nice bonus for my loyal workers in the making." Bebe winked. *Now that's what I'm talking about.*

Boy Wonder came through on our two-way radios. "Hey, Bebe... The strippers are ready to start their next show. Can you get down here?"

"I'm on it. How is everything going down there?"

"Off the chain. Looks like your girls are making mad tips, and I've gotten more propositions than one man could handle in a life time," he laughed. "Y'all been holding back on a brother, but that's okay 'cause I will definitely be back next year."

"Glad to hear that." She turned her attention back to Royce and me. "Are you two straight?"

"I'm offended," Royce teased, before Bebe playfully hit his arm.

After Bebe left us, Royce took advantage of the opportunity. "Nikole, are you sure you're okay?"

"I've been better, but hey, I can't complain." I finally let down my emotional guard. I told him about my conversation with Dr. Williams.

"That's great... I think? But are you okay? I mean, weren't you considering keeping the baby?"

"Actually, I was going to make you go with me to the clinic on Monday, but now that won't be necessary. I guess it wasn't meant for me to have a baby, or an abortion." I touched my stomach as an unexpected wave of loneliness washed over me.

"It's going to be okay, Nikole. Trust me." He paused before asking his next question. "So, what's going on with Jackson? Have you heard from him?"

"I tried to call him before I came over here, but I guess he's still pissed off with me about the whole Terrance and Mercedes drama."

"Can you blame him?"

"No, I can't, but..."

"Honey, take it from me. If he cares, he'll call. Shit like this is never easy."

"Don't get me wrong, I was really feeling him, but I will understand if he decides to go his separate way." I began to sniffle.

"Yeah, right," Royce deadpanned, with his usual sarcastic response. "So, what's up with you and Brian?" He looked around to make sure Bebe hadn't snuck up on us. He leaned in closer as I continued to spill my guts.

"I haven't seen or heard from him. You know, he didn't even show up this morning to bail me out of jail, which didn't surprise me."

"Now I would have been shocked if he did show up. What about Mr. Pretty Boy?"

"Who, Terrance?"

"Hell, I don't see any owls up in here. Who else have you been sleeping with?" He teased.

I rolled my eyes at Royce, "My daddy told me that Mercedes was already in trouble with the law for harassing the woman that I saw Terrance with at the restaurant. So right now they are probably knee-deep in legal matters, and I am sure I'm the last person on his mind. But as far as I'm concerned, from now on our relationship will only be centered around Omar and his well being."

"That's how it should have been in the first place." *Too bad it took me all of these years of heartache and drama to figure that out,* I thought to myself.

"Changing the subject, what's up with you and Charles?" I redirected.

"Shit. He decided he wanted to be hetero again, and I decided it was time to do me. Anyway, I met this fine brother name Emanuel the other night. Girl, he is *luscious.*" Royce fanned himself.

"It must be nice."

Royce cleared his throat. Someone had grabbed his attention. "Now why would a fine brother like him be in a place like this?" His eyes had diverted toward the bottom of the staircase, but before I had a chance to follow his lead Bebe interrupted us.

"Royce, no flirting," She had returned to our side via her back stairwell. She wore the goofiest grin on her face as she sashayed into the balcony area to join us. I wondered why she was looking like a love struck teenager. My question was quickly answered when Brian appeared behind her. He was all smiles, too.

"Excuse me?" I tried to hide my disappointment behind a fake smile. "What are you two doing together?" *I bet that smile on your stupid face is the reason you left my ass in jail overnight!*

"A whole lot," Bebe's smile grew wider. "You're going to be an auntie." She took my hand and tried to place it on her belly, but I pulled away and looked her straight in the eyes. *That low down, no good... Ooohhhh, I hate his ass!*

"When did all of this happen?"

"I took a pregnancy test this morning, but I just told Brian. Isn't this great!"

"Excuse us, Brian I need to talk to my friend for a minute." I pulled her arm, moving us out of his hearing range.

"Sure, take your time." He smiled mischievously before stepping to the side to speak with Royce.

"Girl, what is going on?" I whispered.

"I just told you, we're having a baby."

"But I thought you said that he was cheating on you, remember? Pictures don't lie."

"Well, that's in the past. Besides, Brian promised that he's going to act right this time."

"So, that's it."

"He's my husband, Nikole. What do you expect me to do?" She searched my eyes, a little longer than necessary, if you asked me.

"Oh my goodness...Bebe..." I stammered, speechless.

"Just be happy for me, okay."

I was at a loss for words, but she never noticed as she continued to babble non-stop.

"What made me so mad was that every time I brought up the idea of us starting a family, it was never a good time. Then he went out and made a baby with another woman. But now," she paused, rubbing her stomach. "Things are going to be different. This is what we needed. This baby will make things right between us." she smiled.

My reeling thoughts wouldn't allow me to partake in her happiness. I had a burning question that I desperately needed to be answered first. "Bebe, why did you do it?" My face showed my utter confusion.

"Why did I do what?" She stared at me with this absolutely clueless expression on her face.

"I know about the magazine that you sent to Mercedes, Bebe."

That's when the most evil smile began to spread across her hideous face. It was as if she'd been waiting for me to ask that question all along. "You know what they say, Nikole."

"No, remind me." I waited for the other shoe to drop.

"Keep your friends close…"

"…And your enemies closer," I completed the phrase for her in a whisper.

"See, I finally figured out why men cheat, Nikole. Men don't cheat because they can. *No, they cheat because of bitches like you.* See, you've got it all wrong. Women think that they're using men, but in reality, you're the ones getting played. All you are to men like my Brian, Terrance and Jackson is a good time and an easy lay, with no strings attached. They *never* marry women like *you*." She let that marinate for a minute as I gawked at her. "Instead, they just *fuck you*." She spoke through clenched teeth, with that evil smile still stretched insanely across her face.

"You ain't nothing but a *sideline ho*, Nikole." Her grin grew impossibly wider. "You never meet their mothers. You can't call them at home. They never take you out in public… Guess why? Because you are their whore," She stood taller as she continued to insult me.

"I sent that magazine to Mercedes so that it would get back to you. Make you realize that somebody else was fucking your man behind your back." Her eyes narrowed. "I wanted to make your life a living hell, like you've made mine."

"You fucked Terrance?!" My hands curled into fists, but I fought to keep my anger in check. *This bitch was sinister.*

"I see why you hung in there with him for so long. He really is a good fuck." She gave her bun a proud pat, and then the smile disappeared. "After tonight, this friendship is over with. Do you hear me? Take your paycheck, and get the hell out of my life."

I stared at Bebe in disbelief, shocked that my old high school friend had found the nerve to do what she had just admitted to me. I'd had a lifetime to get used to being trifling in my ways, but I never imagined Bebe having the heart to do all of this shit. *Who did she think she was, trying to go toe to toe with me? Didn't she know who I was?* Everything in me wanted to knock her conniving ass down the damn staircase, but at the last minute, I decided to just let that bullshit go.

How in the world could I fault her for sleeping with my Terrance, who wasn't really mine in the first place? After I had done what I had to her household, I had no right to blame any body else for anything they did to get back at me. Lord knows I didn't need any additional drama in my life at this point. Truth was, we were both wrong. Hell, *everybody* was wrong, and there wasn't a damn thing that we could do about it now except move on, and count the causalities along the way. I would be lying if I claimed that I wasn't still ready to throw down for what she had done, but like I said before, it came down to karma. She had made her point, and I had no choice but to accept it. Besides, after tonight, our friendship never would have been the same anyway. I couldn't trust her, and she damn sure couldn't trust me. In all honesty, she never *could* trust me, even from the beginning. I swallowed the boulder in my throat as Bebe held my eyes with hers, and knew that this was the end.

"Hmmm, excuse me. I hate to break up the love fest that you two are having, but I think Nikole has a visitor." Royce interrupted, thankfully.

"Royce, no one is here to see me."

"Does the name Jackson sound familiar?" Royce grinned.

"He's here?" As I nervously looked over the balcony to search for him, Bebe and her confrontation disappeared from my mind. *What could Jackson possibly want? After yesterday, there wasn't anything left between us. Isn't that what he had said? I was nothing but a whore. Wasn't that what Bebe just called me?*

"In the flesh, honey." Oblivious to the standoff between Bebe and me, Royce pointed at the bottom of the stairs excitedly, and this time I allowed my eyes to follow his hand. I took a deep breath and tried to walk, but my feet refused to move. *What if he sees me as just another freak? What if he's here with someone else? I can't take that right now.*

"Nikole, girl, you better get down there, and get your man!" Bebe nudged me with her hand as if the tongue-lashing she'd just given me a few seconds ago had never taken place. Brian had returned to her side, but the look on his face told me that he didn't share in Royce and Bebe's enthusiasm over Jackson's appearance.

"Please," I shrugged my shoulders, pretending not to care. I realized that Bebe really was good at faking a front. No wonder she had been able to fool me this entire time. She had me thinking that she didn't have a clue about my relationship with Brian, and the entire time she was fucking Terrance behind my back. And with the snap of a finger, she had gone back to pretending to be cool with me. *Unbelievable.*

"Girl, if you know like I do, you had better get your uppity ass down there and resolve what ever happened between the two of you before somebody else up in here comes along and snatches him up." Royce snapped his fingers with his signature attitude.

He had a point. Deep in my heart, I couldn't deny that I wanted things to be right between us. It had only been twenty-four hours since we'd last spoken, and I missed him already. I put Bebe behind me, leaving the three of them on the balcony and making my way down the stairs.

As I approached Jackson, he looked just as nervous as I felt.

"What are you doing here?"

"Looking for you. Got a minute?"

"Yeah, sure," I nervously replied. As we headed outside, I caught a glimpse of Royce smiling down on us. "Did he call you?" I asked Jackson, gesturing to my best friend.

"I'm taking the fifth," he smiled as he looked up and waved at Royce conspiratorially.

Leading me to the pool area of Bebe's estate, Jackson took a seat on one of the lounge chairs and motioned for me to join him.

"I've been thinking about you," He moved my hair behind my ears and nestled his face next to mine.

"Really?"

"I know I said some harsh things the last time we were together."

"Hey, I was wrong for not being up front with you about the pregnancy."

"Yeah, well, I'm not going to sit here and act like that scene yesterday didn't bother me because it did. That whole fiasco just fucked with my head."

"Well, Jackson, no matter what happens between Terrance and me, he is still Omar's father. For the record, my relationship with him is now officially past tense. I realize now that I was wrong for getting involved with him and allowing him to hit on me, but I think that entire gruesome experience has taught me some valuable lessons about myself. Also," I took a deep breath, "I'm no longer pregnant. The doctor called me and told me that I had an abnormal pregnancy. It's a long story, but the gist of it is that there is no baby. Never was."

He took a deep breath as he wrapped his arms around me. "Damn, Nikole, I'm so sorry."

I nodded, looking into his eyes and seeing his sincerity. I couldn't think of anything else to say. I had said it all.

"Nikole, I missed you."

I leaned back, my head resting on his chest. "So, what are you trying to say, Jackson?"

"Can we pick up were we left off, minus the drama?" He turned my head toward him, and placed a gentle kiss on my lips.

"I think I'd like that," I touched his hand and returned the kiss.

Normally I Don't Do Shout Outs But....

This is the part that I like!

First and foremost, I would like to give thanks to the Creator, because He gave me the strength to see this project through despite all of the obstacles that were placed in my path.

Next, I would like to thank my beautiful sons, Jorden and Taye. Words can't describe how much I love you guys. Thank you for the unconditionally love and keeping me grounded 25/8.

To my parents, thanks for all of your love and support throughout the years. Thank you for pushing me to try new things and for making me step outside of my comfort zone as a shy kid. It is because of your tough love that I am the woman who stands before the world today. I miss you so much, Mama, but I know you'll always be with me in spirit.

Big Brother Wil, what can I say? Thank you for being you, for having a sista's back when necessary and for always keeping it real no matter how it will make me feel.

To my friends and partners in crime: April White, Germaine Gordon, and Michael Gatson, what would I do without you guys? You just don't know how many times you were my lifesavers when the world was weighing a sista down! Thank you for always seeing beyond C.J. and accepting and appreciating the true me.

To my Aunt Jeanette, thank you for the phone calls just to say hello and to make me smile across the miles. You'll always be my #1 auntie!

Special thanks to my writer friends Anna J, Byron Harmon, Dr. Ivory A. Toldson, Vanessa Johnson and Naiomi Pitre for being my mentors.

To my line sisters, those Devastating Divas of Delta Sigma Theta, Baton Rouge Delta Alumnae Chapter, Spring 02, always keep your heads up and your right foot forward.

Last, but not least, thank you, the reader, for believing me... It is because of you, you and you that I write!

About the Author

CJ Domino is a native of Baton Rouge, Louisiana and a graduate of Southern University and Tulane University. The award winning writer currently resides in her hometown where she serves as CEO of Shero Productions. A member of Delta Sigma Theta Sorority, Inc., CJ enjoys traveling around the world as a motivational speaker, using her background as a clinical social worker to inspire and uplift women from all walks of life.